Odd Ball

Odd Ball

Arthur John Stewart

thistledown press

Thistledown Press Ltd.
118 - 20th Street West
Saskatoon, Saskatchewan, S7M 0W6
www.thistledownpress.com

Library and Archives Canada Cataloguing in Publication

Stewart, Arthur John, 1951-
Odd ball / Arthur John Stewart.
ISBN 978-1-897235-88-1

I. Title.
PS8637.T4942O44 2011 jC813'.6 C2011-901713-X

Cover and book design by Jackie Forrie
Printed and bound in Canada

Canada Council for the Arts Conseil des Arts du Canada

Canadian Heritage Patrimoine canadien

Thistledown Press gratefully acknowledges the financial assistance of the Canada Council for the Arts, the Saskatchewan Arts Board, and the Government of Canada through the Canada Book Fund for its publishing program.

To S, D&A
My editors in all things that matter

Prologue

We all had a working sixth sense once. By we, I mean our human ancestors who were alive eight-hundred-thousand years ago. That extra sense told us things that our five other senses couldn't detect. One of its main jobs was to stay in close touch with the faintly-whispered messages sent out by nature: it's safe to sleep here — don't hunt in that direction — the sky may be clear but a storm is coming, seek shelter. That extra sense came in handy to help us survive. We discovered that it was great for reading other people and that we could actually use it to help us find a friend to dance around the campfire with.

Believe it or not, we still have that extra sense. It's buried inside our big brains, mostly sleeping now, like our tonsils, appendix, and spleen. What happened? Why would we ever stop using such a great tool in our lives? No one really knows for sure. One theory is stress. Stress can sometimes override all the good things the human brain can do, the kind of stress caused by war for example.

Whatever caused it, when we did lose our extra sense, the world became a darker, lonelier and scarier place.

Then, sometime during the Middle Ages, some smarty-pants wizard or sorceress — which is what research scientists were called in those days — came up with the idea of trying to find a way to get back in touch with our lost sense even though absolutely everyone thought it was long gone. And, surprisingly, the smarty-pants found a way. Through trial and error, he or she discovered the power of a colourless rock mineral known as beryl. Although beryl is clear when pure, it is nearly always tainted by impurities. Those interior imperfections dance and change shape when flickering candlelight shines through the rock. Something about the process of looking into that stone managed to put people — at least temporarily — back in touch with their dormant extra sense. And in almost every case, what people who experienced that contact wanted to know about, was how to find a friend to dance around the campfire with. The process of looking into the stone became known as scrying, or seeing direction into one's future. Sometime later, scryers discovered the effectiveness of the more powerful mineral, crystal. When it was shaped and polished into round balls or orbs and used for the same purpose, the scrying process became known as crystal ball gazing.

As years went by, other materials were found that would help people make contact with their extra sense — black glass, polished quartz, emerald, and reflecting elements such as a water, oil and mirror surfaces. As more and more people were able to access their extra sense, more and more of them were able to find their way to the only future that really matters to us human beings — love.

Slowly, but surely, the world came out of its darkness.

Unfortunately, as science grew more popular in our society, the art of scrying lost favour. Being invisible to the naked eye, the ability to contact our sixth sense was difficult to prove. Besides, who dances around campfires anymore? Thus, no longer considered necessary, scrying has all but vanished from our world, remaining alive only within a few stubborn people who still believe it has a place in our lives.

Despite all of that, the extra sense continues to be passed down via our chromosomes and glows, however faintly, within us — in the anterior cingulate cortex to be exact. It's possible that you may even have noticed it — — a feeling or sudden awareness that something or someone is trying to get your attention; but when you look around, everyone is either wearing ear buds, talking on a cell phone, sleeping, or trying to figure out what the teacher is so excited about. Yet, if you took a second look, you'd probably notice a decorative glass orb sitting on a shelf, or perhaps someone near to you wearing a crystal pendant, or an antique mirror hanging on the wall — or maybe even one of those shiny toy balls, the kind that gives odd answers to yes or no questions. Although all of the above are ordinary items in our everyday lives, they can also act as mediums through which our deeply buried extra sense is still trying to do its job, to contact us with important information — about an approaching storm or maybe, about someone nearby who would be just perfect to dance around the campfire with.

Dumb Question
Ask Another

Kevin

I notice Jobbi the day he first shows up at Central Middle School, almost a year ago. He's standing alone in the main hallway directly between the bathroom doors. I'm standing nearby, waiting for a friend. A girl. I also notice Pinger coming my way so I take off my glasses before he can knock them off. He isn't interested in testing the unbreakableness of my glasses again, though. That's because he also notices the new guy.

Pinger has muscles, a moustache, and an entourage. He keeps his followers entertained by making fun of kids who aren't strong enough to fight back, and that includes just about everybody. He announces, "Hey, who's this new guy?" Jobbi doesn't seem to realize that Pinger is talking about him.

"Oh-oh. It looks like he might have blanked out." Pinger changes direction slightly and gets close enough to rap Jobbi hard on the back of the head with his knuckles. "Hey, Newbie, wake up!"

Jobbi grabs the back of his head and squeals, "Aakveyaya! Leeksmimira!"

The whole entourage laughs. I have to admit that I do too. I've never heard anyone react like that to being hit. Later, I learn that Jobbi isn't from Canada, but somewhere in Europe. He actually speaks three different languages, but unfortunately, none of them is English or French. He is standing between the bathrooms because he isn't completely sure which door to use.

That treatment of Jobbi doesn't stay funny for long. Not to me. I've been dealing with bullies forever. Everyone always thinks I'm a geek because I wear glasses, get good grades and suck at sports. I'm not, though. It's a well-documented fact that real geeks are too shy to talk to girls, especially pretty ones, but I talk to them all the time! Three girls I know would probably even say that we're friends, and I think one of them, Dawn, might even consider being my girlfriend, although Jobbi doesn't think that's a good idea — but that's a whole other story. So, even though I'm clearly not a geek by definition, I was still the number-one bully target in our school — until Jobbi arrived.

The bullying of Jobbi continues for the rest of that whole year and into grade eight. At least once each day you hear someone yell, "Hey, Newbie, wake up!" That's followed by a whack, then Jobbi's squeal, and finally, loud bully-chuckles. By the start of the next school year I can tell that everyone is tired of it — everyone except the bullies that is.

Unfortunately for Jobbi, he also has this awkward habit of standing right in the middle of a busy hallway, lost in thought and staring at the wall, with his mouth slightly open. For bullies who happen to come across him in that state, it's like an open invitation for them to do their thing. Fighting back only makes things worse for Jobbi, the biggest problem being that he doesn't know how to fight. Most of the grade-eight boys can probably hold him off with one hand. And it doesn't help that he only weighs fifty-five kilograms even though he's fairly tall, or that his arms and legs look like toothpicks.

All in all, I think I have to describe Jobbi as really gangly. He has short, dark hair that's constantly scattered in every direction, even when he tries to gel it into submission. He wears the same, neatly ironed, white dress shirt and brown corduroy pants to school every day. A wide black belt that overlaps itself by half, holds his pants up high enough to allow the pointy toes of his shiny black boots to show from below his wide pant legs. He has unusually long hands that are matched by long feet.

I see right away that Jobbi is going to be a popular bully target, so I get to know him and try to teach him a few basic survival strategies, like how to walk unnoticed beside — yet slightly behind — passing teachers, how to slip into an empty hallway locker before an approaching enemy can spot you, and about staying away from groups of girls when the silverback bullies are around. I got that name from a library book about Western Lowland Gorillas. The Silverbacks are the meanest bullies and they never miss an opportunity to humiliate their victims whenever they're found in the presence of girls. The more girls there are around, the more important it is for the bully to demonstrate his dominance.

Jobbi and I eat lunch together in the Geek Safe Zone and signal one another when we sense trouble in the area. It isn't a proud existence for us, or anyone like us, but it is basic-middle-school-survival-for-those-who-can't-fight-back.

I think trying out for the hockey team is a way for Jobbi to fight back.

Get A Clue

Stephanie

Jobbi's in a couple of my classes. I notice him, but he doesn't seem to notice me or any other girl for that matter. And it isn't until second period science, two months into grade eight, that I start to figure out what's different about him. Me and Rena are late for class that day. We duck in just before the teacher closes the door, only to find this new, sort of chunky Asian girl sitting right in Rena's desk! The girl's name is Soon Lee, but no one knows that yet. Everyone in the class has their regular seat and I can see that the new kid senses that we're all staring at her. But she won't budge and just keeps looking straight ahead, all kinda nervous-like.

My friend, Rena, is this really, really tough girl who has tons of confidence and always gets what she wants one way or another. The whole class is waiting to see what Rena's going to do about this kid in her seat. My personal guess is that she'll scream, "Outta my desk, bitch!" — then grab the new girl by the hair and throw her across the room — or something like that. It so happens that Rena is in a good mood and she just stands behind the girl, casually chewing gum and looking around at everyone with this funny/crazy look on her face, letting us try to imagine what's coming. Then, before Rena can do anything, that strange, skinny guy, Jobbi, who I've been wondering about, stands up and says, "Rrreenah, vill chyou pleece tew hove mwy diesk?"

Everyone is, like, "Whaa! What is he thinking!? There's no way in this world Rena'll take his desk, not way on the other side of the room! OMG, he'll be lucky if she doesn't go over there and slap some serious sense into him!"

And that's definitely my first reaction too, but then it strikes me — why's this guy, who's normally super quiet and happens to be a bully punching bag himself, mixing it up with the toughest girl in the school? I mean, what does he care about this new kid? Isn't it humiliating enough for him to be constantly beat on by Pinger and his entourage? Why would he take a chance on getting punched in the face by a girl, like George Snead who accidentally stepped on Rena's foot during square-dancing in Phys-Ed?

Or . . . did Jobbi know something. Something that no one else knew — not even me?

Rena glares at Jobbi, like she can't believe what he's said to her, all the while blowing a bubble with her gum. It gets bigger and bigger and bigger. Pop! Everyone freakin' jumps. Then she says, real sweet-like, "Okay, Joobie. I'll take you up on that."

Huh?! So Jobbi scrambles across the back of the class to an empty desk in the far corner, and Rena saunters over to his, all the while giving the new girl a look to let her know that she didn't do this for her and she better be really careful in the future about whose desk she sits in.

Even our teacher, Ms. Docktroff, is standing there all stunned with her mouth open. And now I'm pretty sure that weird skinny guy does know something. So, later that day,

I wait for him when he exits from his hideout in an empty hallway locker.

"How did you know?" I ask before he even knows I'm there.

"Aakveyaya!"

He always makes that noise whenever he gets surprised by someone and I so totally surprise him by being there.

"Stayfusplurk?"

He also seems kind of flustered for some reason. Like, more than normal.

"It's ok. You can tell me. How did you know? C'mon, c'mon, Jobbi."

"Eyes-sklilp-pa?"

He appears to be tongue-tied, the way guys get when they talk to a beautiful girl, like say, Cheryl. But there's only me here, so his stammering doesn't make much sense.

"Jobbi. You sit behind Scott Chalmers. Somehow you knew that Rena likes Scott — even though she's never told anyone that except me."

"Eatvuzahhuhh?"

"You knew she'd take your desk when you offered it to her because of Scott, right?"

"Purhumm-ma-baa."

I don't know if anyone actually understands Jobbi. His crazy accent and coming from a different country make everything about him seem a little weird. I think that's what actually interests me about him. I suspect there just might be more there than meets the eye. For instance, I didn't even know that Rena liked Scott, not until after that class anyway. That's when Rena actually told me.

"Admit it. You didn't want to see that new girl get hurt, did you?"

"Yeznn . . . chousu . . . saury"

I squint at him like he has something real small and hard to see on his face. But I'm also checking out his enormous, dark eyes, long, dark lashes and thick black eyebrows. He looks at me as though he's trying to see inside my head because he isn't quite sure exactly what I'm talking about.

"How did you know, Jobbi? Never mind. Don't tell me. I'll figure it out."

I back away slowly until I get around the corner. Once I'm out of his sight, I hear him hyperventilating as though he's been holding his breath the whole time. I might be the first girl to talk to him outside of a classroom since he arrived from Latvia a year earlier. I think he handled himself quite well under the circumstances.

I've read about these people who are supposed to have some kind of mental abilities. They can somehow sense other people's emotions. I wonder if Jobbi is someone like that. He doesn't seem to understand what I was getting at regarding Rena and Scott. Yet, he really took a big chance. He must have figured something out.

I have an aunt who can draw people's faces perfectly, using only a fat marker pen. She can do it better than most of the stuff you see in art shows. It's easy for her, like doodling. Still, she doesn't feel there's anything special about it. I wonder if Jobbi could be like that. Able to do that ESP thing and not even realize how unusual it is?

What Do You Think?

Soon Lee

I regret the dishonour that I have brought upon my father for being sent away from the private school his company provided for me. He is very angry and wishes to send me back to Korea to live with my grandparents. My mother has somehow won a reprieve for me. She knows there were some difficulties at the school. It was impossible for me to keep the bruises hidden completely from her eagle eyes. She doesn't know of the daily torture I suffered at the hands of other Asian girls who felt my Korean-Filipino heritage was disgusting to them. They claimed it was my abnormal genetics that explained why I was not reed-thin like them. Being strong and stubborn like my father has never been an advantage to me. I fail to run away when I should do so. In defending myself from my tormentors I broke the nose of a girl. Without thinking I lashed out with my elbow as she was spitting insults into my ear. An ambulance had to be summoned to take her to the hospital.

My mother was a singer of renown in Manila. Marifel. My father, a Korean engineer, was sent there to renovate a factory for his company. He hired my mother to sing at a party for visiting company executives and their wives. They fell in love and married on the day before he was to return to Seoul. My mother had some medical problems when I was born and was unable to have more children. She tells me that she is not unhappy about that at all because she already had what she wanted most — a daughter. We lived in Seoul until I was eight, at which time we moved to Singapore. My father completed his work there just after I turned twelve, but instead of returning to our home in Korea, he brought us to Canada, where he is now overseeing the construction of a new factory. Because we've been away from Korea for so long, he insists that our family try to live in the traditional Korean manner while we are here. My mother, who loves her new life as a Korean wife, spends all of her day frantically overseeing renovations to our apartment and training the domestic workers to do things in the Korean way.

In all of my schools — Korea, Singapore and now Canada — I have made only one friend. When I was seven, I met a boy who wore glasses and was terribly clumsy. He made me laugh, and when I laughed, he laughed with me. I was teased harshly by classmates over my friendship with him, but I didn't run away. He invited me to his eighth birthday party which was held at his home. The day after the party he told me that his parents asked him not to be friends with me anymore — that I wasn't a Korean. He told me he didn't want to listen to what they said, but soon afterward, he was moved to a different class, and after that to a different school. I never saw him again.

In Singapore, an older Taiwanese girl from my school — who also enjoyed pop music — became my friend. The girl invited me to her home, introduced her parents to me and even invited me to a sleep-over party. The following weekend the girl asked if she could visit my home. My mother was excited that I had finally found a friend. The girl arrived at our home accompanied by her own mother who carried a large fabric bag. Inside the bag were scrapbooks, pictures, audio tapes, CDs and videos . . . of Marifel. The girl's mother had been a huge fan of Marifel's during her teenage years. My mother was pleasant with the woman and with her daughter — for my sake — signing all of the paraphernalia they requested and even posing for photos with the two. I was asked to hold the camera and take the photos. My mother turned down an invitation for her and my father to attend a party at the woman's home, saying she no longer attended such functions — which was true. The woman became insulted and left. My friend lost interest in me after that visit.

My schools have always been private and expensive. In such places, who your parents are always decides your popularity with the other kids. As most kids had never heard of my mother, my parents were not considered to be wealthy or popular. It was, in fact, the exact opposite, because I was of mixed race.

I very much like pop music and know all of the most popular Korean, Singaporean, Chinese, Filipino, British and American female singers. I listen to them on my Apple computer and visit chat rooms with other people like me who love that music. No one there knows that I am Korean-Filipino. I don't think anyone cares. We just enjoy discussing the music of our favourite singers and sharing what we have heard about their private lives. It is fun. I sometimes wish I had a friend nearby who I could go out to the shopping mall with or to the movie theatre or a concert and have some fun with.

Despite the disorder I have made of my life at my last school, I still believe that there are other kids who are like me — and like the ones I chat with on my computer. Perhaps they don't go to a private school.

Yesterday I went for a walk in my Canadian neighbourhood. Not very far from where I live I discovered a large, square, old building with the words *Central Middle School* in worn out lettering above the main doors.

Sure

Valmiera, Latvia

Before coming to Canada Jobbi, his mother Taska and his father Taylus (Tay-ous) were living in the town of Valmiera in the Northeast of Latvia, near the border of Estonia. Taylus owned a small plot of land just outside Valmiera. It was an inheritance from his father and he harvested peat from it. The peat was shipped by train to St. Petersburg, where it was then sold as a cheap winter fuel and burned in brick or stone stoves.

Taska worked in the largest hairdressing salon in Valmiera. She was popular among the older women who could afford her skills as an aesthetician. The family enjoyed life in their small apartment and could even afford accordion lessons for Jobbi. Then, without warning, peat fuel was banned in St. Petersburg when city officials became concerned that its heavy smoke contributed to an already dangerous air-pollution problem. The distributor was forced to cancel his contract with Taylus. It was a serious blow to the family.

Taylus wasn't able to find another distributor. He tried to sell the land, but it wasn't fit for anything else and no one was interested. Although Taylus tried hard to find other work, he found only low-paying, temporary positions. By being very careful with their money and cancelling Jobbi's accordion lessons, the family was able to keep their apartment and get by.

One day, at the salon where Taska worked, talk among the women turned to memories of her grandmother, Indra. Most of the older women in Valmiera remembered Indra with great reverence. Some of them even considered her to be the saviour of their town. One of the women at the salon that day swore that Indra had possessed true second sight.

"She had only to look at a man or a woman to know exactly what his or her heart yearned for."

The legend of Indra was that she could have done anything with her power, even made herself rich, but instead, she used her ability to help lonely people find love by becoming a matchmaker.

The Second World War had been very cruel to Latvia and to Valmiera in particular. Many thousands of its residents had died or been taken away, first by the occupying Soviet army, then by the occupying German army when they drove out the Soviets in 1941. Most never returned. Many were women, but even more were men. Indra's own husband was forced at gunpoint to join the German army in April, 1943, then sent north by train with many other townsmen to fight the Soviets. The conscripted Latvian soldiers were driven directly to the front line of the battle and most were killed.

Indra's husband never returned. She was left to care for her three young children. It was a dark time for everyone.

To survive after the war, Indra searched through the burn piles left by the fleeing soldiers. Then she and her children cut, dyed and sewed the various shreds of the hated uniforms, tents and bags they recovered, to create somewhat stiff, yet extremely warm and durable blankets. They would sell or trade them at a vibrant outdoor street market that sprang into existence when the war ended.

The men of the area who did return after the war had nothing left. They were forced to take work as labourers in the fields and barns of the farm collectives in the surrounding area. These farm labourers became Indra's main customers. Although they almost never paid her with currency, they did have lots of fresh farm produce which they were willing to trade generously. She managed to feed her children and keep their home.

Late in the evenings of those post-war years, to prevent herself from despairing over the fate of her husband, Indra put her mind to the needs of her many customers. She personally knew numerous women who had been left alone by the war, and it was clearly as right as rain to bring lonely individuals together to enjoy whatever happiness remained. As difficult as that time was for Indra, she persisted in her belief that there was love to be found if one knew how to find it. And sure enough, love bloomed. Again and again, Indra's matches proved to be remarkably accurate. It was not long before men found themselves working a little harder and with more purpose, and the women found themselves having babies.

As for Indra's method, she couldn't believe the fuss people made over it. To her, it was less about deductive thought and more about listening to what her intuition told her. Her method was to simply observe her subjects. She tried to find moments when they weren't aware that she was watching them. The very best time for doing that was at some supremely quiet moment, when a woman or man was alone, idly looking out at the world. It was then that Indra was able to discern her subject's true desire. Rarely, however, did that sublime moment actually reveal another person who would be the perfect match for her subject. Instead, Indra remembered many, many of those unobtrusive observations. Then later, at unexpected moments, sometimes while she slept, sometimes as she went about her daily business, occasionally in the privacy of the toilet — and always as a complete surprise — an exact match, one for the other, would reveal itself. To Indra, it felt like finding the solution to a complicated problem. She never doubted the absolute truth of these unexpected revelations.

Of course, there was always the chance that the two individuals involved in these insights might somehow find their own way to one another, as two people meant to be together often did. However, as far as Indra was concerned, there was far too much at stake to sit around and wait. Her philosophy on the subject was simple. "The sooner the better."

When it came time for action, Indra rarely approached the two subjects directly. Her best and easiest route to making a successful match was to involve one or both parents and/or grandparents. Grandmothers were best. The rest was easy. She preferred semi-accidental encounters, over the awkwardness of forced, formal introductions. Through her suggestions, these encounters were arranged and sometimes rearranged, opportunities such as shopping at one or the other's usual market or coincidental strolls along the river, or Indra's favourite — sending one, by *accident,* to the address of the other with flowers for an ailing friend of the grandparent. The confusion would often lead to a combined effort in searching out the correct address of the recipient. Ultimately, with much less encouragement than most conspirators would imagine, the new lovers would soon be seeking out places where they could be together and happily alone.

Indra's daughter, Thalia, had also grown up with *the eye*, as the people of the region called this particular skill. And although it was a much less desperate time, Thalia felt a duty to her community to encourage the matches which were so clearly obvious to her. With the help of these two special women, Valmiera grew and prospered after the war.

Then Indra passed away. She had never married again — as was the case with any true matchmaker. Thalia first spoke to her future husband the day following her mother's funeral.

Sadly, everything changed three years later when Thalia gave birth to Taska, her only child. It was a difficult pregnancy and Thalia passed away from complications following the birth. Many of the women felt that the good fortunes of their town died with her.

Taska had heard many of these legends from her father, but had never considered doing any matchmaking herself, until Mrs. Liepa told her about what her Grandmother Indra had earned for those important services of bringing men and women together, "who should be together!"

"Without ever asking, a generous honorarium would appear the day following the wedding ceremony — usually from the bride's parents, but sometimes from both sides. There would be another generous honorarium on the first anniversary of the marriage, and a smaller 'remembrance' each year after from the happy couple themselves. That's not all. No, no, no. There would also be a fat gift of money from the wife's parents, the husband's parents and the couple themselves to celebrate the first child who was born. Yes, Dearie. A Matchmaker with a good eye could earn herself some very generous gratitude. Do you not agree?"

That's Ridiculous

Kevin

The notice in hallway F that catches Jobbi's attention is about the tryouts for the school hockey team. I know what he's thinking — that if he makes the team, the bullying and insults will stop. True, but the problem is that it's a grade-nine team and we just started grade eight. Plus, the same jerks we spend all day trying to avoid are all going to be on the ice with him. I'm Jobbi's best friend and I don't want to see him get hurt. I tell him straight out, "Don't even think about it, Jobbi." He doesn't listen. Five minutes later, we're in the Phys-Ed office. The teacher in charge of sign-ups looks at Jobbi's slim build and shrugs. He tells Jobbi that he will be allowed to try out for the team if he shows up.

Jobbi's mom gave him a new hockey stick for his birthday. I think she believes that's what a boy needs in Canada — to fit in with the other kids. She's probably worried that Jobbi isn't fitting in all that well at school. He isn't, but I know for a fact that he never complains to her about it. She has enough worries of her own.

For skates, he borrows a pair from his cousin Victor — goalie skates that are too small and have blades that look like they've never been sharpened.

Jobbi had told me once that he played a little hockey back in Latvia — not Canadian-style hockey exactly, but on the river with his father, his friends and some neighbours, including three girls. He says the game they played was more like team figure skating than hockey, because the three neighbour girls, and one of his friends, all dreamed of becoming world-class figure skaters. They only agreed to play hockey with him so they could improve their skating strength. Apparently, the figure skaters, who had had some real training, combined the two different styles by doing things like jumping high into the air to escape being body-checked, and spinning like tops on one skate before taking a shot on the goal. Being only an average skater, Jobbi says he had a hard time keeping up, but really liked watching the beautiful skaters. I guess they played often and Jobbi learned how to dart in and out of scrums quickly and to get his stick on the puck while the other players posed dramatically for an imaginary crowd, or paused to bow deeply and gracefully after making a particularly clever play.

When it comes to the school team tryout, though, it doesn't look good for Jobbi. I want to see what's going to happen so I go along with him to the tryout, but as soon as we get to the rink, Mr. Bauer, the school caretaker, sees that I'm not carrying any equipment and hands me an armload of orange pylons to take out to the players' bench. He keeps me busy giving him a hand with all the equipment stuff that he looks after for the team, but I'm still able to keep my eye on Jobbi and the other players. I count forty-two of them getting dressed in three different changing rooms. Every player there has previous competitive team experience and all the equipment you're supposed to have to play. Jobbi has neither. Coach West takes one look at him sitting in the dressing room wearing his goalie skates, hunter hat and nylon ski gloves, and informs him that he can't let him on the ice without the proper equipment. The coach sweeps his hand around to the other players in the room, which includes the gigantic, grade-nine bully, Pinger Shumzicky.

"Just like the other boys here are wearing."

I can tell that Jobbi hears the other players snickering and making sarcastic comments about him. I also know that the comments that hurt him most are the ones that make fun of the way he speaks.

"Cane ahhi goa at duh toilot Teashur?"

"Doe nut tu hit mea plizz."

"Kayveen, hawear du you goa?"

Jobbi gets a lot of that, kids making fun of his accent. I find it kinda weird because I probably talk to him more than anyone, and I never have any problem understanding him. It's the kids who know him least that make the most fun of him.

Mr. Bauer gives me the keys to the dressing rooms so I can lock the doors after the players go on the ice. When the buzzer sounds, announcing that the ice is ready, Jobbi, for some reason, gets up and follows the others out. I'm curious about what he's up to. Just outside the room, he's stopped by one of our teachers, Mr. Dixon, who is helping Coach West with the selection of the players.

"I'm sorry, Jobbi. You can't go on the ice dressed like that. It's for your own protection, son."

Jobbi nods, acknowledging our teacher's words.

I try to sound sympathetic. "Too bad, man. You tried." I'm actually secretly relieved that we're going to get out of there before any of the real nasty bullies have time to pay attention to us. The place is absolutely crawling with them. "I'll lock the doors and give the keys back to Mr. Bauer. Then we can go home."

But Jobbi doesn't move. At the very last second, just before the rink attendant completely closes the gate, Jobbi hops onto the ice. I can't believe that he's gone out there with absolutely no equipment on. I lock the dressing room doors and hurry back to watch.

All forty-two of the players trying out for the team are circling the ice counter-clockwise. They're wearing every colour of helmet, sweater, hockey pants and socks you can imagine. It's impossible to pick out someone you know in all of that confusion — except if that person happens to be Jobbi. And it's not his equipment — or lack of it — that makes him stand out. It's the way he skates. He doesn't skate low and balanced like an experienced player. Instead, he skates with this bouncy stride, each push-off lifting his hat-covered head higher into the air, all the while trailing one or the other leg sort of gracefully behind him. When it comes to unusual skating styles, his is hard to miss.

I can see in Jobbi's face that, just for the moment, he's forgotten all of his school and family problems as he sails over the smooth ice, enjoying the cool arena air and the speed he generates with every stride.

Then, suddenly, out of nowhere someone yells, "Hey, Newbie, wake up!"

Before Jobbi can prepare himself, someone knocks him off-balance from behind. He falls to the ice, sliding head first into the boards. It's hard to tell how badly Jobbi is hurt. He isn't moving.

Not A Chance

Brandon

They called themselves the 8-2-5 Gang, but almost everyone downtown called them the Bens. That's because at one time, long before Brandon got in, there were three guys named Ben in the gang. Weird. They mostly did shoplifting — small things they could sell or trade for smokes. They did all their stuff during rush hour when stores were busiest, either in the morning or the afternoon — eight o'clock or five o'clock — eight-to-five? In between those times, they hung around downtown having fun.

Bandon met Zef at the arcade. They were both really good at shooters. They played a single game of Halo 2 that lasted an hour. After it was done they went out on the street for a smoke. Zef had lots of smokes. He kept them in old decks — du Maurier, Players, Export A. Not all of the cigarettes inside the packs matched because Zef traded for them with stuff he lifted: package of three golf balls, three smokes — bottle of aspirin, seven smokes — Slayer T-shirt, fifteen. Brandon thought he was a pretty cool guy. They hung around for a while. Then Zef said it was time for him to go to work. Brandon asked to go along. Zef said, "Sure, why not."

Zef told Brandon to wait outside this restaurant that had a sidewalk café. Two seconds after he went in, he came flying out with a bottle in his hand. It happened so fast Brandon wasn't ready. He just stood there frozen. Then this giant, bald Chinese guy came running out, but when he saw how far ahead of him Zef was, he gave up and turned on Brandon. Somehow he knew the two of them were together. He grabbed Brandon by the arm and dragged him into the lane so the customers sitting outside couldn't see. Then he backhanded him right in the face. Brandon saw stars and fell back into a bunch of cardboard boxes that smelled like rotten meat.

"Tell your friends that if I ever see them around here again, I won't call the cops — I'm going to catch them myself and do a lot worse than I just did to you." Lying there, all Brandon could think about was how the blood from his bleeding lip tasted. "Got that?" He kicked him, but not that hard. After all, he hadn't done anything.

Brandon knew where Zef had gone. The Bens hung out in the basement of a parking garage. Whoever owned it tried to close off the basement section, but there was a way in between the concrete wall and this dusty steel fence — if you weren't too big. The Chinese guy would never have fit.

When Brandon got there, the 8-2-5s had already finished off the bottle of wine Zef had lifted. He told them about the Chinese guy. They all laughed like crazy at what happened. Zef spoke up for him. "He's not too swift, but he wants to join." Everyone stopped laughing and looked at the biggest and oldest guy there, the one and only remaining Ben.

"Uh, thanks, but no thanks. We don't need a crybaby who's going to pee his pants every time he gets caught by some dick." No one argued, one way or the other, not even Zef. When Ben looked at Brandon and said, "Get lost," he left.

By the time Brandon got to the corner, Zef caught up with him again. Brandon could tell Zef was feeling bad about what happened to him at the restaurant. "Ben'll change his mind. You gotta prove to him that you won't rat anyone out. I've got an idea."

They walked to the military surplus store, went in and looked around. When Zef saw what he was looking for, he signalled Brandon to go back outside where he told him his plan. Zef then went back in alone. Brandon watched him through a window and when Zef gave him the nod, he went in too and waited beside the tools counter. A few minutes later, the store's door alarm sounded. Zef had slipped a magnetically tagged store item into a pocket of someone's backpack. When the person went to exit the store, the tag tripped the alarm. Two store employees rushed to frisk the woman carrying the pack. That was Brandon's signal. He grabbed something from behind the counter without looking, then walked quickly to the entrance door Zef was holding open with his foot. His heart was racing out of control, but Zef was giving him this big, stupid smile. With all the commotion going on at the exit, nobody in the store had even noticed him. They disappeared around the corner.

Brandon knew it was a knife he'd grabbed, but he was so nervous he had no idea which one. When Zef saw what it was, his eyes opened wide. "Whoa. That is . . . so . . . cool." Brandon was holding a brown and white, rough-bone handle. It was about as long as his hand. At one end was a curved lever that sort of looked like the trigger of a small gun. When he pressed it, a long, shiny, pointed steel blade instantly snapped out of the bone handle. The blade was thin, and even without touching it, you could tell that it was deadly sharp. They both knew this knife had only one purpose.

Zef bought them a sub sandwich and lifted a bottle of juice to go with it. They went to the playground to eat and stare at the knife, eventually taking turns releasing the blade and thinking out loud about how they'd use it.

"Ben will freak when he sees what you boosted. No store dick is gonna screw with you, dog. Not if you flash this."

Zef was right on. Ben completely changed his mind about Brandon. He joined the 8-2-5s.

About a week after that, Brandon got picked up at the Silver City arcade by the police. His school called his home about him not showing up and his mom called the cops. He didn't know why she did that — maybe the call from the school reminded her that she had a son and that she hadn't seen him in a week or more. She told the cops she thought Brandon was travelling with his dad. He was a transit truck driver.

Brandon could take or leave school. It was no big deal. He mainly joined the 8-2-5s so he wouldn't have to go home. His mom drank most of the time. When his dad was home his parents fought — seriously. Either way, he didn't want to be there. The only reason he ever wanted to go home was to check on his little sister. She was in grade one — or two. She knew how to go over to the neighbours when the trouble started at home.

The cops took Brandon home and told him that if he didn't stay there and go to school regularly, he'd be handed over to Child Welfare and end up in either the youth detention centre or foster care. Zef was in foster care. He hated it — except for some old woman who treated him okay once when he was eight or nine. He still went to see her even though she didn't do foster care anymore. He lifted food for her. Brandon didn't want to end up like that.

Brandon's old school didn't want him back so they changed him to a new school — Central. He went just enough to keep the cops off him. He showed up at home most nights. His dad was hardly ever there and his mom never bothered him as long as he brought her cigarettes, and got his sister off to school so she didn't have to get up and do it herself.

Brandon's new school was a joke to him — everyone pretending it was going to do something for them. But nobody knew when that was supposed to happen. It definitely wasn't the real world. The way he saw it, the Bens were real life.

Ben asked Brandon if he could borrow his knife for something he had to do. Brandon didn't want to let him use it, but Ben was the leader and the guy who had the last say on who was in and who was out. He got the knife back from Ben the next day, and when he looked closely at the opening where the blade went in and out, there was something stuck on the edge. It was dried blood. Zef told him that Ben had gone to meet some guys from the suburbs who had some weed to sell. Ben thought they might try to rip him off. He was right, but when he pulled the blade, they backed off. One of the guys decided to chase him, obviously thinking Ben wouldn't use the knife. The guy was wrong, and ended up with a stab wound in the leg. Ben left him lying on the sidewalk.

Brandon didn't really know why he took the knife to school. Maybe because he wanted the other kids to know that school wasn't his world — that he had another, better life. After math class, the teacher was standing by the door. He noticed the leather case on Brandon's belt. The case was originally a birthday present to his dad. It came with this crazy multi-tool thing in it, for emergencies, but his dad never used it. The knife fit perfectly into the empty case.

The teacher — with a smirk on his face — asked Brandon if the special case was for his hole punch, like he was some kind of book nerd or something. Brandon flipped the case open and showed him the handle. He was definitely impressed and held out his hand, wanting a closer look. Brandon wanted him to know that he wasn't a nobody — like everybody else around there. As soon as the teacher touched the trigger, Brandon realized that he'd made a huge mistake. The teacher got this shocked and serious look on his face. For a second, Brandon thought about grabbing it back, but he might have put up a fight — and who knew how that would have ended up.

"You're not supposed to have something like this at school."

"Can I have it back, please." Brandon said please, but he really wasn't asking.

"No, no, no. I can't give this back to you. Do you know you could be expelled for bringing this to school?" The teacher pressed the trigger again, retracting the blade and then, scared as hell, looked up and down the hall to see if anyone else had seen it. "I don't want you to get expelled, Brandon, but I definitely cannot give this back to you." He looked straight into Brandon's eyes to see how he was going to react. Brandon was worried, really worried, but decided to play it cool because that would probably be his best chance of getting the blade back. He shrugged as though it was no big deal and that there were lots more of those where it came from. It was Tuesday. The teacher said that he had to think about what to do, and that Brandon should come back and see him on Friday at three-thirty.

Ben freaked. The kid he stabbed was in hospital and almost died from blood loss. His parents were rich and connected enough to get all the television and radio news channels talking about street violence, gangs and how it wasn't safe anymore for innocent kids like their son to go downtown with friends to see a movie. The police knew about the blade and were looking for it. They all knew that no matter how much they tried to clean it off, there would still be traces of blood for the police to find if they got their hands on the knife.

Brandon told Ben that the teacher wouldn't do anything with it until he talked to him on Friday and that the teacher would probably keep it in his desk until then.

Ben, Zef and Brandon decided to break into the school on Thursday night. At two in the morning, Brandon threw half a brick through the classroom window and climbed in. They knew an alarm would be set off and that they only had a little time. Zef went to watch the street for them while the other two searched the desk. Brandon gave Ben the pry bar but the drawer wasn't locked, and there was no knife inside. Zef yelled, "They're here . . . one black and white."

It was only when Ben and Brandon were climbing out the window that Brandon realized they were in the wrong classroom. They all looked the same at night. He decided not to say anything. Outside they didn't see Zef. The three of them had planned an escape route through the trees behind the school to a road with a big culvert under it they could hide in. Ben and Brandon started heading that way when they heard Zef call to them. There was a single vehicle in the back parking lot — an old Dodge pick-up. Zef was inside sitting behind the wheel. "Why run?" he said. Then as the truck started up, " . . . when we can drive!"

Who Cares

Paula

I'm not quite sure how, but all of a sudden there were all these kids out to get me. I didn't think it was a good idea for me to just stand around and wait for something to happen. I'd learned from my mother that people all have their own problems and you need to look after yourself. No one's going to do it for you.

In my first week at Central school, a little over a year ago, someone told me this story about a teacher who disarmed this kid who was threatening him with a knife. The guy was in a gang and not long after the teacher took his knife away, the kid was killed — probably because he didn't have it for protection when he needed it. This all happened quite a few years before I got to Central. I was still excited to see this tough, street-fighting teacher. I remember how disappointed I was when I finally did. Mr. Drew is this small, super-skinny, balding, glasses-wearing guy who is always stroking his beard with his hand while he talks, except that he doesn't actually have a beard, so it's pretty strange. I totally could not believe that he was capable of disarming anybody, never mind a guy from a street gang. Stories can get so exaggerated.

The rumour was that Mr. Drew had kept that knife in the locked drawer of his desk ever since the kid was killed. Some sort of guilt thing. I never believed any of that until I was passing his desk on the way out of math the day before yesterday. He'd left the desk drawer he normally kept locked, open. It wasn't the knife itself I saw, just a leather pouch. For some reason the pouch looked familiar to me. And I don't know how I knew, but I was certain that the knife was inside of it. Without thinking it through I took the pouch from the drawer and put it in my bag.

Once Mr. Drew realized it was gone and told the principal about it, the whole school completely freaked out. They're looking for that knife everywhere. Everyone is convinced that it was a guy who took it. That's good for me. I know I'll be expelled if I get caught with it. But I'm not as worried about that as I am about my life. I need it for protection just as much as the kid Mr. Drew took it from did. Besides, what are the chances they'll figure out that a weak, innocent, little girl has it?

Obviously

Valmiera, Latvia

Taska often wondered if she had inherited the *good eye* from her mother and grandmother. It seemed to her that she should give it a try. After all, what harm could there be in it?

One of her salon customers, Mrs. Jumikis, had a granddaughter who was nineteen. Taska knew of Aija and her wish to go away to the University of Riga in the fall. She was Mrs. Jumikis' last grandchild and the doting grandmother very much wanted the child to stay somewhere close to her in Valmiera. It seemed to be a good case to test Taska's abilities.

She began her research by visiting some coffee houses on her way home from work in an attempt to discover who might be available. She was surprised to find very few young men about. She was confused about this, until a server told her that she should come in later, after the young men were done on the pitch. Football! It made sense. Taska began to visit the pitches. She covered them scrupulously, one or two a night. She was pleased to discover that there were several good candidates available.

One evening, she met an incredibly dashing, well dressed, young Russian by the name of Boris Michalenkov. He was sitting and watching friends because he had recently suffered a knee injury in a car accident. During the conversation, he told Taska that he had spent the last several years wandering the world, but now wished to settle down and was waiting to begin training as a technician at the hydro-electricity plant. He dreamed of one day buying a property somewhere around Valmiera. Yes, a wife was definitely in his future plans, but he admitted to being quite bashful and having a hard time meeting interesting girls. Taska felt instantly certain that she could help him and Mrs. Jumikis. She obtained his telephone number and departed.

On her way home, a tear came to her eye. She now understood why her mother and grandmother had used their gifts of second sight the way they had.

On Mrs. Jumikis' next visit to the salon, Taska brought up Aija. Mrs. Jumikis responded with an obviously heavy heart. "Yes, Aija still insists on going to Riga in the fall."

"Would it make any difference if she had a boyfriend here, perhaps?" Taska inquired.

"Perhaps, but where could a man with enough assets to catch her eye be found?"

"Would you like me to give it a try?"

Mrs. Jumikis' eyes brightened. She knew about Taska's mother and grandmother. She could also tell that her friend had a plan in mind. Together, they worked out the details.

It took two well-planned *accidents* for the young hopefuls to meet — one at a coffee house when Aija and her grandmother stopped for a rest while shopping, and the other at a football match that Mrs. Jumikis suddenly wanted to attend. The relationship caught, and late that summer, Aija and Boris were married. Before the wedding, Aija's father loaned Boris the money to buy the property he dreamed of owning.

Boris' parents were both aeronautical engineers involved in the Soviet space program and worked on the launch of the Soyuz spacecraft scheduled to rendezvous with the Americans at the International Space Station. They sent a telegram with their deep regrets for being unable to attend their son's wedding, but promised that they would visit very soon. They also sent the happy couple a prepaid reservation for a two-week stay at an exclusive resort in Madagascar.

The wedding was celebrated far and wide in Latvia, Estonia and Russia because of Aija's father. He was a member of the Latvian People's Party and a ministerial deputy in charge of ensuring that the trade routes to and from Northeast Latvia remained open and accessible to its neighbours. He accomplished this by encouraging local businesses to participate in fair trade and by dealing very harshly with any and all corruption that damaged those trade relationships. Business owners from miles around Valmiera, sent their tribute to the brilliant, young couple. The wedding was large and lavish.

The post-ceremony reception had to be held out of doors on the property of the bride's parents, to accommodate all the guests who begged to attend. Fortunately, the weather was fair and the eating, drinking and dancing went on under the moon until three o'clock in the morning, after which the newlyweds retired to a guest cottage beside the lake.

Taska, as the matchmaker, her husband Taylus and twelve-year-old Jobbi were among the invited guests. They had a lovely time and sang folk songs on the drive home in the rental car, with Jobbi falling asleep on his mother's shoulder. When the car was quiet, Taska wondered why Aija's mother had not introduced her to Boris and Aija as their matchmaker. She suspected that Inta Jumikis was not yet prepared to tell her daughter that there had been some behind-the-scenes help in finding her Boris, her happiness. No matter. Taska was proud of her work. It would come out soon enough.

Late the next morning, Taylus got up while everyone else in the apartment slept. He went out to buy some biscuits, milk, and aspirin. On his way back, a friend stopped him with some unsettling news. It seemed that there was concern from the wedding site that the groom was nowhere to be found. The gifts and tribute from the wedding had also mysteriously disappeared. The friend had been sent to determine the disposition of the property the groom had purchased using his future father-in-law's money. Taylus rushed home and woke up Taska.

What they didn't know quite yet was that Boris had jilted Aija and stolen everything her friends and relatives had presented to them. The day prior to the wedding, he had quietly sold the property his future father-in-law had financed. The good wishes and airplane tickets from his parents in Moscow were fakes — as were the space-engineer parents themselves. The worst part, as it would eventually be discovered, was that Boris had done the same thing two other times in the previous four years in different locations and under different names. Each time he disappeared, he returned to a real wife and two children north of St. Petersburg on the Gulf of Finland, laden with money and beautiful gifts. Never before, however, had he returned with such a rich bounty.

The implications of Boris' actions were immense for Taska. Not only had Taska's second sight completely failed her, but she was also guilty of ignoring one of the most important functions a matchmaker must undertake — to be doubly sure that the people she matched were legally available to be married.

Taylus had a bad feeling about what conclusions the authorities might draw about Taska's involvement with Boris and what that could mean to their family. Taska felt sick. But they had no time to feel sorry for themselves. Taylus acted quickly. He took his grandfather's gold watch and chain to the pawn dealer, whom he had to convince to open his shop. With the money he received from the watch, he bought two bus tickets to Riga, and put his wife and son on the next bus.

Taylus gave Taska all of their savings, then called his brother in Canada and asked him to send plane tickets for Taska and Jobbi so they could visit him and his family, just until he could figure out what, exactly, the situation was. Taska didn't argue because she knew it would be best for their son. Ten minutes after the bus departed for Riga, an official government car pulled up in front of their apartment building.

Whatever

Stephanie

Okay, so I know school in general sucks, but this place has somehow become a real mess. I don't even know how it happened. It isn't anything obvious — at least not one incident or something that you could point at and blame: The weather is crappy, always grey and raining. The coolest teacher in the school and the only one I ever talked to, Ms. Rambersad, got sick in early October and didn't come back. The best student president the school ever had, Jesse Twerndon, moved up to grade nine and is in the high school section now and our new president, Leslie Krueger, is way too happy and way too cozy with Principal Largebutt.

To make things worse, the real lunchroom is closed for renovations and won't be open again until after Christmas, so we have to eat lunch in the stinky basement multipurpose room. Every time I go down there I feel like some kind of bug that drags its food into a hole in the ground so that it can eat with the rest of the crammed-together, buzzing, munching swarm of other bugs. And, oh yeah, the Fall Dance is cancelled for the umpteenth year in a row.

All that stuff and more just keeps piling up and getting on everyone's nerves. Next thing you know the whole school is as cranky as my grandmother's old, half-blind house cat that hisses at you if you go within six feet of it.

Okay. There've been two big after-school fights involving high-school guys — the police had to be called out both times. And there are sooo many people who don't like other people, who don't like anyone, that it's becoming totally impossible to keep track. And the overall school morale thingy — that just keeps getting worse and worse. It's getting to the point where school is not a fun place to be. And that's really weird, 'cause in the past I've always felt more comfortable at school with my friends than at home with my bizarro cuckoo-bananas family.

And ok, when I walk down the hallways? I only look straight ahead. I feel like if I look right or left, or even up or down, I'll end up making someone mad at me. Lately I've been getting sixties on my tests and hanging around with anybody who isn't upset with me at the moment. Still, of the two, writing tests is almost more fun. And Rena, my longest best friend from forever? Okay. For some reason she's turned into one of the most difficult people to get along with. We totally don't hang out together anymore. Way.

All of this stuff happening this year is a complete shock to me because last year, grade seven, when Jesse was School President, it was completely different. That whole year was so fun. I remember the first thing Jesse did last year was to organize a hallway boycott of all classes on a Friday afternoon. He wanted the principal to reinstate the Fall Dance. Largebutt refused, of course, and threatened everyone with suspensions if we didn't go right back to class. Most of the kids caved and went back, but me and Rena stayed out with about twenty other kids. Then the principal tried to have us all herded into the gym, but Jesse told everyone to lock arms together so we couldn't be dragged away. It was so crazy and totally fun. At the end of the day, when we were leaving, Largebutt told Jesse that the student council was disbanded because of him and that he was suspended from school for ten days. What a jerk. The suspension ended up not sticking because Jesse's parents hired a lawyer. Still, the dance wasn't reinstated and Jesse was cut from the volleyball team over it, even though he was their best player.

Whatever. Nothing the principal did last year to try and get control of us worked, because, in the end, as far as we were concerned, Jesse ran the school. I figured out from watching him that a good leader can really make a big difference. School was actually a fun place to be — last year. For instance, a huge boom box showed up outside the back door by the parking lot next to where all the smokers went out between classes? It played all day, every day, even in winter — and someone was always dancing out there. Sometimes things went crazy and there were ten or twenty or even more kids rocking out.

That was last year.

This year, there is no boom box and no dancing. And, just when everything seems so completely hopeless, out of nowhere another crazy thing happens, and it involves that Jobbi guy again. One day, we get this substitute teacher in Phys-Ed class. She doesn't have a clue about what to do in our gym period, so she asks us what we want. I say volleyball because it's the only sport I can play without looking like the complete sports dork I am. Anyway, for some reason that I still don't get, the sub asks Jobbi to pick the teams. Everyone in the class groans really loud to make the point that Jobbi is not at all a cool choice. And yeah, maybe he isn't that cool, but I'm interested to see what he'll do.

Sure enough, instead of the girls at one net and boys at the other, he divides everyone into mixed teams, three girls and three guys on each. He does it so fast that no one has a chance to complain. Suddenly I'm having the most fun I've ever had in Phys-Ed. Really. And I'm not the only one who's having fun. We play for the whole hour and when the bell goes for lunch, we all ignore it to finish the game. The sub is grinning from ear to ear and no one seems to know what just happened.

But I do.

Jobbi somehow figured out a way to pick teams of kids who would get along together. In fact, some of the kids were even more than just friendly, if you get what I mean? Jenny Franks and Lawrence Nobiss, Rena and Scott, and Jeremy and Ricki. My team was pretty cool too. It was really nice to see everyone having some fun for a change.

Forget About It

Paula

My real dad split from us for good after my brother died. He was older than me by six years. I remember him less and less every day, like he's a part of a strange dream that's slowly disappearing from my memory the longer I'm awake. My mom and me lived in a mobile home for a long time after my dad left us. Then she married Michael, my stepdad. It was when we moved in with him that I started at Central Middle School.

Starting at a new school isn't that bad as long you don't think about it too hard. The fitting-in part is all that teachers, parents and counsellors can talk about. "Just learn to fit in, dear. Fit in with the other kids and everything will be fine."

It doesn't seem to matter to them if fitting in makes you feel sick or ugly, or like hurting yourself. As long as you do it, they're happy. That's because they want to believe that if you fit in, school will immediately become this incredible paradise full of good friends, great teachers, fabulous classes and everyone accepting you for who you are.

Right. Maybe that was the case fifty years ago when they went to middle school, although I doubt it. Whatever — it's definitely not what fitting in means now. In this school, it means doing whatever you have to do to *not* get noticed, making sure that everyone sees that there is absolutely nothing special about you, and hating yourself just as much as they hate themselves.

If you can't, or won't make yourself completely invisible by fitting in properly, then you end up standing out, like a gigantic, flaming-red, chin boil, and that makes you a target for every bully in the school — from the obvious, big, punchy ones to the sneaky, small, soul-destroying ones, and all the others in between. And when you don't fit in, then school is about as far from a paradise as you can possibly get.

I know how to fit in — teeny-bopper Keds, wide-legged black denims, dark hoodie, straight, vegetable-dyed burgundy hair, long bangs over as much eye makeup as I can get away with wearing. I never look anyone in the eye or speak above a loud whisper. My overall look was just like the other girls in my grade. In some ways, fitting in is like wearing this safe, cozy, bully-proof coat. It works because hardly anyone even knows you exist. I used to be ok with that.

At least I thought I was.

Yeah, Right

Kevin

Even Jobbi agrees with me about geeks. There's no way you can be one if you have a girlfriend — and I almost had one. The difference between a girl who's a friend and a real girlfriend, is asking her. I mean, if I want a girl to be my girlfriend, I have to ask her if she wants to be. When I say *I almost had one*, I mean that I'm pretty sure Dawn would say yes if I asked her. She's really nice and friendly, gets good grades, and she wears glasses, just like me.

I know what everyone thinks — that if my girlfriend's a geek, that would mean that I'm a geek too. Umm, sorry. I don't think so, because I know lots of geeks and none of them can talk to girls, not even if the girl is a geek too — unless they don't even know that their geek friend is actually a girl, which happened to Devon.

Me and Devon are walking between classes with our friend, Alex, and talking about what is and isn't CGI in the new Terminator movie? Anyway Devon's arguing with Alex about whether you can actually see trails from laser weapon fire when all of sudden, they're both gone. I look around and the next thing I see is Devon sneaking out of the girls' bathroom.

He had followed Alex all the way in not realizing that he's walking into the Girls' or that Alex is short for Alexandra.

A geek gets really nervous and jittery around girls. But I am not — and never have been — anything like that! I'm actually very funny. Funny enough that I can make girls laugh — not at me, but at a joke. I also look right at them when we're talking, although I don't see them that clearly because I need a new prescription for my glasses. I do drop things all the time, but not because girls make me nervous. My mom says I'm fidgety. I've always enjoyed taking things apart and putting them back together.

Getting back to Dawn — now that I think of it, she's not a geek either. She plays volleyball on the school team. I went to see one of her games. She did sit on the bench most of the time, but she got to play a little and looked really good in her uniform. Unfortunately, she got hit in the face by the ball when a big girl from the other team spiked it right at her. Dawn didn't have her hands up and the ball broke her glasses. It must have hurt too, because Dawn cried. I don't think she noticed that I was there to see that.

I would ask Dawn if she wants to be my girlfriend — if it wasn't for Jobbi. When I first told him that I liked her, he says, "Dyoo vaunt tew merrry disgarrrul, Daoon?" So I explain to him what a girlfriend means. It means you talk to her in the cafeteria after you finish eating lunch with your friends, you walk her part way home after school, and you can call her about homework if you miss something. He looks at me with this really strange, sort of perplexed look and says, "Sooo disgarrrul, forrr yoos, Kaveen, nahsomahtch." Not for me! I don't understand how he can say something like that. He doesn't even know her. He only knows what I told him about her. Jobbi seems pretty sure about her not being the right girl for me, though. He shakes his head at everything I say to try and get him to understand how wrong he is about her. He won't budge. In the end, I put off asking her until I finally see that Jobbi might be right.

Jobbi and I live on the opposite ends of Hillcrest Street, so after school we walk down Simpson, which is the street that runs into Hillcrest about halfway between our houses. We meet there in the mornings too, on our way to school. Sometimes on the way home we stand on the corner and talk for an hour. We talk about everything, but mostly about what went on at school. Sometimes I ask him about Latvia and he asks me about some of the television shows that he doesn't understand — not the language stuff, but things like, "Why do the aliens on *Star Trek Voyager* all look like humans wearing masks?" or, "Why doesn't Buffy the Vampire Slayer know it when her friends are possessed?" And then I say, "Yeah. And why doesn't Mulder ever kiss Scully when everyone can tell that she's totally in love with him?" Jobbi's head snaps up and he just looks at me, but I can tell what he's thinking. "Oh c'mon Jobbi. I know you watch *X-Files*. You must see it. The way she looks at him? She totally loves him."

"Mmm porrrahps."

"What?! But . . . Just ask anyone! She's nuts about him!"

"Mmm. Nooa. Hiya doan booleeves somahtch."

"What? Wow man. I don't get you sometimes." He just shrugs.

Well, Maybe

1142 Hillcrest Ave.

When Victor graduated from Central High School, the only thing on his mind was getting away from home, as far as he possibly could. He was five when his father brought the family to Canada from Latvia to work as a machinist with a company that a friend of his had started. Victor's sisters were four and six at the time. The three of them grew up as Canadians, speaking like their friends, dressing like their friends and thinking like them too. Their parents, however, hardly made an effort. They spoke English well enough to get by at their jobs, but at home it was always Latvian, Latvian, Latvian, as though they wanted to try to live the same life they did in Latvia even though they were now in Canada. Victor and his sisters were not in the least interested in the old country, but that didn't stop their parents from telling them about it constantly. Victor even dreamt of it sometimes, although the dreams often took the shape of nightmares, because he didn't remember a single thing about that country.

Victor and his sisters spoke English to one another and only spoke Latvian when their parents forced them to. And they were good at English. They actually spoke better

English than most of their friends who were born in Canada. That's because they worked hard to fit in with their friends. Victor's parents could have done the same if they didn't spend all of their spare time with people from the local Latvian community. What really bugged Victor and his sisters, was that their parents were always speaking Latvian to them in front of their friends — as if that's what they spoke at home. It made them feel like they didn't really belong in Canada, and never would, as long as they were living at home.

When Victor got to high school, he figured out that if he studied hard enough he might have a chance to get away. It worked. He received three scholarship offers during his grade-twelve year. He chose the university that was furthest from home by convincing his parents that it would provide the best opportunity for him to become a computer engineer. That, by the way, was his parents' dream — not his. But he was willing to do whatever it took to get out of there and give himself a chance at a life he wanted.

His sisters hated that he got to go and they didn't. The truth was that they could have left also if they had wanted to. They both did well in high school, better than their brother, in fact. The difference between them was that both sisters had serious boyfriends near home. Victor had a girlfriend at university he hadn't told anyone about yet.

It was when he was packing to go back to university for his second year that Jobbi and his mother arrived from Latvia. His parents were ecstatic of course, and he too was happy to finally see these long-talked-about relatives from the old country in person. Jobbi and Taska hugged each of them as though they were their saviours. Standing in the front yard of his home with these visitors, Victor found himself glad — maybe for the first time in his life — to be able to understand the language his relatives spoke and to be able to respond to them — at least in partial sentences. That feeling caught him by complete surprise. Later, he figured out that despite having lots of Canadian friends, they did not have any actual blood relatives in Canada.

Jobbi and Taska were worn down by their fifteen-hour flight and they both looked exhausted. It didn't take much to figure out that the flight wasn't the only thing bothering them. Their faces were marked by concern and fear. Taylus, Taska's husband and Jobbi's father, had been left behind under very uncertain circumstances. They obviously feared the worst for him. From what Victor overheard, their situation back home seemed clearly unfair. Suddenly, he felt that he wanted to protect these unfortunate relatives who seemed powerless to defend themselves from harm in Latvia. He wanted to use all of his Canadian knowledge and wealth and strength and everything else at his disposal to help them correct this obvious injustice. How could he have known at the time that it would be them who would change *his* life?

Oh, Please

Paula

Cheryl Fehr didn't fit in and never had. We were walk-between-classes friends only. She showed me around when I first arrived at Central but we didn't hang around much outside of it. I learned that she didn't have a mother and had to take care of her nine-year-old brother and seven-year-old sister whenever her father wasn't around — which was nearly always.

Cheryl hardly ever smiled. She did really well in all of her classes and didn't care that she stood out. When someone picked on her, she just ignored the bully, as though she had more important things to worry about.

This one day, we'd just written a test and I'd dropped mine on Mr. Herman's desk on the way out of the classroom. He was a young, sort-of-nervous-and-twitchy-but-cute guy. Cheryl was after me and I watched while she tried to give Mr. Herman one of her rare smiles as she was leaving, but he didn't look up at her. She was lucky that even without smiling she looked pretty.

Sometimes I think that I might be pretty, but I'm not really sure about it. How am I supposed to know anyway?

I'm definitely not super skinny, not even close, and I'm not tall like a fashion model. My mother doesn't look like a model either but she's pretty. That's why Michael married her. They go to a lot of parties together. Michael seems really happy to have her.

No one outside of my family has ever told me I'm pretty. In fact, it's just the opposite. Every time I begin to think I might be, and start to believe in myself just a little bit, someone will make it their job to bring me down and put me back where everyone else is at my school — hating themselves. Since the start of this school year, I've been called chunky buns, stunned bitch, precious, heavy chick, trailer twerp, bug eyes and maybe worst of all, skinny mini — that was said sarcastically by one of my teachers, a man. It's as though people can't stand it for a single second if they get any hint that you're feeling good about yourself.

You Wish

Stephanie

Okay, I had no idea that Jobbi had gone to the hockey tryouts. When I got to school that day, the first thing I saw was Wally Shumzicky and his grade-seven dufus buddies running around the hallways with toilet paper wrapped under their chins and tied in a big knot on the top of their heads, like some kind of old-timey bandage that people with a sore tooth used to wear. Wally is Pinger's younger brother and if it's even possible, more obnoxious. He isn't as big as Pinger — yet — but it's pretty clear he wants to follow in his big brother's footsteps as a nasty bully. I have no idea what the toilet paper is about, but I know it must have something to do with making fun of some poor kid. Wally is definitely one of the reasons that school is as bad as it is. He can get away with doing whatever he wants because everyone is so afraid of his brother. The complete freedom to bully anyone, at any time, has gone to his head — and it's a pretty stupid head to start with.

I've been thinking a lot lately about what Jesse Twerndon would do if he were here this year. It's hard to figure out exactly how he made school so fun last year. And even if I did figure it out, I know I'm not a natural born leader who can do the same things that he did. The truth is that I'm almost the opposite of Jesse when it comes to getting attention. I'm small and tend to be mostly quiet when I'm in a big group — although I do get kinda yacky in a small group and with my friends. My dirty blonde hair does attract some attention, but I'm pretty average in the looks department. All in all, I'm not the kind of girl that gets noticed. I'm more of a watcher, really. I'm also smart enough to see when something is wrong. And there's definitely something wrong around here.

I don't think I can to do much on my own, but I'm pretty sure I could be of help to someone who *can* do something — someone with brains and courage and character — maybe even someone who doesn't realize how strong and influential he can be. I could help somebody like that . . . and I actually have the beginning of a plan in my head. That's when I see Jobbi come slumping down the hallway toward me. His head is hanging down and he has what looks like an oversized chinstrap on his face, the kind you use to keep a football helmet on your head.

Most of the time, I can't tell how Jobbi is feeling because he's really good at being quiet and hiding things. This day, though, he isn't hiding anything. He looks completely miserable. His 'chinstrap' is made out of three long pieces of white adhesive tape strung across his chin to hold two thick, spongy bandages in place. It almost covers the bottom part of his face from just below his lower lip. His cheeks on either side of the bandage are quite swollen too. To make matters worse, Wally and three of his goof buddies are following Jobbi, imitating his shuffling kind of walk and sticking their toilet-papered chins in the air.

"Jobbi, what happened?" He doesn't even get a chance to answer me.

"My brother creamed him into the boards at hockey practice last night. They had to carry him off on a stretcher. Ha. Ha. Ha." The goofs all laugh and hold their heads in their hands and stagger around as though they're dazed. Jobbi turns and glares at Wally. Wally immediately mocks Jobbi's look.

"Oooh. I'm scared."

"GET LOST YOU LITTLE TWERPS!" I say it so loud that they're all shocked — for about a second at least. Wally immediately sticks his sneering face in mine and I realize that he's actually five centimetres shorter than me. "Shrimp."

"Dyke."

That was the first time anyone had called me that name and it catches me by surprise; but I also realize that he said it because he's intimidated by me and doesn't want any of his buddies to know that. I lean forward and whisper to him, "You've got some guy stains on the front of your pants." I turn and walk away while Wally checks his crotch. As I round the corner, Wally yells something at me that I don't catch. Probably a good thing I didn't. Jobbi vanishes. I knew that he would.

In math class, Kevin tells me that his sister hears that Jobbi's father is in prison. Kevin thinks it's in Latvia. It has something to do with a wedding. That doesn't make any sense, but Kevin really doesn't know anything more, except that Jobbi's mom went back to Europe to help her husband and left Jobbi to stay with his cousins.

"No wonder Jobbi looked so not good."

"No kidding, Steph — I went to watch the hockey practice, just to see how Jobbi would do. I saw Pinger knock Jobbi down from behind during the warm-up. He fell pretty hard and without a helmet on he hit his chin on the ice and split it open. I rode to the hospital with Jobbi and Mr. Dixon. It took eight stitches to close the cut. I heard the coaches talking together before we left the rink. They're really worried about being held responsible for Jobbi's injury because he was on the ice without any equipment. They think his parents will make a complaint."

"He didn't have *any* equipment?"

"Only a stick and skates. No helmet, kneepads, gloves — nothing."

"No way!"

"Way."

"Are his aunt and uncle going to sue the school?"

"I doubt it. My dad picked us up at the hospital emergency ward and we dropped Jobbi off at his house. He wouldn't tell his aunt what happened even though she was freaking out. He just kept saying that he was all right and that he was tired. I don't think his aunt and uncle even knew about him going to the tryout."

As If

1142 Hillcrest Ave.

Jobbi was excited to meet his cousins for the first time, and to be in Canada. Victor's parents were even more excited to have a reason for everyone to speak Latvian together. That lasted about a day before the kids started to speak to Jobbi in both English and Latvian. That was soon followed by speaking only English. Jobbi let them know that he liked it better that way because he wanted to learn English, and in all honesty, his cousins' Latvian wasn't very good. He picked up English quickly, at least as far as the understanding part went. He treated learning it like a game — a form of charades with words. Victor and his sisters found him fun to be around. He brightened up the house with his energy, despite how serious the adults remained. Victor left for university a few days after Jobbi and his mother arrived, but he called home every weekend and came home every two weeks for clean laundry.

Jobbi and Taska were only supposed to be in Canada for a short visit, a week, perhaps two. But two weeks soon became three and the short visit eventually became an extended one. Jobbi and his mother slept in the basement bedroom and lived and ate meals with the family upstairs. As time passed, the small house grew even smaller. Jobbi's uncle and aunt never complained or said anything to make their visitors feel unwelcome, but the family knew that Jobbi and his mom were concerned about intruding on their lives.

Every day, Taska sat by the telephone waiting for her husband Taylus to call with news that she and Jobbi could go home. But after two months, Taylus reported that the situation in Valmiera was still not safe for them. And so, because they didn't know when they might be returning, the adults all decided that Jobbi should start school in Canada.

Victor and his sisters weren't so sure. They guessed how freaked-out Jobbi would be about going to a new school, in a strange country, two months into the year and speaking very little English, but he didn't complain. His parents had much bigger problems to worry about and he didn't want them worrying about him.

Jobbi's understanding of English was actually quite amazing for the short time he'd been there, thanks to constant coaching from his cousins, but he remained very self-conscious about speaking the language. Because they had also gone to Central School when they were younger, they knew that most kids there were pretty cool and would try to help Jobbi out. There were going to be some kids, however, who definitely would not make life easy for him. Those were the ones that he had to worry about.

Victor's parents were convinced that with Jobbus being as smart as he was, he would learn Canadian English more quickly at school. Taylus was also sure that sending Jobbi to school in Canada was the right thing to do. Taska was not as certain and was clearly worried that she might be feeding her son to the North American wolves. As things turned out, her concerns were justified.

It was unfortunate for Jobbi that not one of his cousins still attended Central School. Starting something new is always easier when someone will show you the ropes. In this case, Jobbi was strictly on his own.

Ask Me If I Care

Paula

One morning before school, while I was eating breakfast, I noticed my stepbrother staring at my chest. I was wearing the same old Sugar Ray T-shirt I always slept in. He'd come to live with us recently because there'd been problems with him staying at his mom's — something about not getting along with her new boyfriend. Whatever. He was seventeen, on the heavy side and a total mess. He'd dropped out of school and didn't get along with his real dad, my stepdad. He was supposed to be looking for a job, but he mostly sat in the basement TV room watching talk shows all day.

My mom must have noticed Dylan staring at me too because, after he left the table, she spoke to me without looking up from the papers she was reading.

"Don't come down to breakfast dressed like that anymore, Paula."

"Yeah, right. Whatever."

"Pardon me?"

I made a heavy sigh. " Yeah, right! What about you?"

"Me? I'm not the one parading around the house with my chest pushing through an old threadbare T-shirt."

"Well, not when you're at work anyway."

"At work? What's that supposed to mean?"

"I see the way Michael gets you to dress when you go out together." She seemed surprised.

"I dress the way I like. Michael has nothing to do with it." She was looking right at me and I could tell she had more to say but didn't.

"He wants you to look hot."

"Don't be ridiculous, Paula. I might be dressing a bit younger lately. But that's not for him."

"He wants you to look like a s . . . "

Before I could finish the word, my mother slapped me in the face. It shocked me and my cheek burned. I covered my face with my arm for protection in case she took another swing. But it didn't come. When she spoke, her voice was quivering.

"Don't you ever say that word to me. Do you hear?" I didn't answer. "Do you hear me?" She was screaming. I thought she was going to hit me again, so I nodded and forced out an, "Okay!" She gathered up her work papers angrily and left the house.

After my brother died and my real dad left, we moved into this trailer park. I was in grade two. Every day she walked me to school and every day she was waiting when I came out. She watched what the other girls in my class were wearing and got me whatever was popular even though we couldn't afford it. We read books together and she helped me with schoolwork even when I didn't need it. We were really close. The problems came when she went to parent/teacher meetings. If a teacher said anything bad about me, my mom went crazy and treated me like I was this hopeless case who was going to end up dropping out soon if she didn't fix the problem right away. I had no idea what the teachers said to her because, as far as I knew, I was almost perfect at school. I thought my dad might come back if I was.

One day in grade four, my friend Jenny missed school because her cat died. Some boys made fun of her when they found out. I was with her when she was being teased. For some reason she turned on *me* and told me that my brother died trying to escape from the police. She said he was in a stolen truck that crashed into a building. Her dad is a policeman and had been involved in the chase. I asked my mom about it. She got really upset about me finding out how my brother had died. She met with the principal and the school counsellors and stayed really upset for a long time. She cried a lot. Eventually she stopped drinking, found a job, and things got a lot better. Then she got together with Michael.

I knew it was a terrible thing that I'd said to her about how Michael wanted her to dress, but I also knew that she would never have hit me if things were ok between them. There must have been something going on I didn't know about and she was worried about losing him. The last thing she needed was me interfering and making things even worse by telling her how desperate I thought she was.

I didn't really understand my mother. I thought we'd been doing fine on our own.

I know what people like to say — like mother, like daughter, right? I guess that's true, because I do sometimes find myself wondering whether anyone will ever want me.

What Do You Think?

Stephanie

Since Jobbi's injury at the practice, Wally is so on Jobbi's case, real hardcore. It's pretty difficult to stand by and watch — not just for me, for everyone who sees Jobbi getting pushed around by that little jerk.

Ten days or so after that, when Jobbi's bandage finally comes off, we're walking down the hallway and the hockey coach, Mr. West, stops Jobbi to tell him that even though all of the players for the team had been chosen, he would like to give Jobbi a real chance to try out.

"But don't forget, Jobbi. We can't let you on the ice without the proper equipment. We don't want you falling and getting hurt again. Come to my office and I'll give you a list of everything you'll need."

I know the coach did it to make sure that Jobbi wouldn't complain to the principal. I don't think Jobbi would have anyway, but whatever, they were willing to give him a shot. All right.

Jobbi's spirit has been improving as his injury has been healing, but later that day, I see that he's totally hanging his head again. He's holding the hockey equipment list from the coach and he knows there's absolutely no way he can get all that stuff by practice time that night, even if he had the money — which he doesn't. Kevin has some soccer kneepads in his locker and I have a pair of skater elbow pads, but that's not much help, because the coach had warned Jobbi that he needed everything on the list.

Okay, so it looks pretty bad for Jobbi, but then I, Stephanie so totally save the day. To be honest, it was more of a coincidence really, but that coincidence might just have saved the day for all of us.

In Your Dreams

Kevin

I can't believe it. He's going to hockey practice with no equipment — again! "Why, Jobbi?" I say. "There's no point. They definitely won't let you on the ice. And even if you manage to get on, the players are going to kill you!"

All he has is the same stick with no tape on it and those old goalie skates. It's crazy, worse than that even — complete suicide. You couldn't drag me into that dressing room even if I was covered from head to toe with bulletproof SWAT armour. I have to stop him somehow. I grab his arm. He just shrugs me off and walks in like he has nothing to live for anyway. Mr. Bauer is there and signals me over to him. I watch as Jobbi takes the first spot he sees on a bench, sits down and starts putting on his skates. The other players nudge one another and nod toward Jobbi. Pinger, who's sitting right across the room from him, rolls up a piece of used sock tape into a ball and throws it at Jobbi as he's bending over his skates. The tape ball hits Jobbi on the top of the head, but he ignores it. Pinger indicates to the other guys, with hand signals, that they should do the same thing. A couple of them start to make their own tape balls.

"Hey, Vanderhof, either get in there or move your fart arse out of the way." It was Jesse Twerndon. I'd forgotten he was on the team too. I move the puck buckets Mr. Bauer gave me to carry out. Jesse plops his big hockey bag down right in the middle of the dressing room.

"Hey, Jobbi. Here's the stuff I was supposed to bring for you."

He opens the bag and starts throwing out kneepads, gloves, socks, a jock strap, a Chicago Blackhawks jersey — everything a player needs and Jobbi doesn't have.

"Some of that might be a bit big 'cause I borrowed it from my old man, but those are my skates from last year. Try 'em. I've got big feet. They'll probably fit you better than those dull things."

Only Jobbi and I can see Jesse wink. It's good that he did because until then, Jobbi doesn't realize what's happening. But he finally gets it that someone is helping him out.

Personally, I'm not that surprised because Jesse is the kind of guy who does things like that. Helps people out. I know that almost everyone wishes they could be like him.

I'd like to help out kids who could use it sometime, but it's not that easy. I mean, most kids don't want your help even when you offer it to them. Somehow, Jesse is different. Everyone just trusts him.

Jesse sees what's going on with the tape balls. Before he sits down, he stands in front of Jobbi and waits until the players give up on the idea.

As for the actual hockey practice, that doesn't go so good. Jobbi doesn't know any of the drills and the ones that he does figure out, he can't really keep up with. His hockey skills aren't great, especially when it comes to anything that involves body contact — which in hockey is everything. He constantly keeps himself well away from the puck and from any player who wants it.

I sit with Mr. Bauer near the players' bench and notice parents in the stands pointing at Jobbi and making comments about his weird skating. Some even laugh out loud. And to be honest, his skating is unusual. Fancy-dance skating would probably be the best way to describe his style. When Jobbi wants to go fast, he just kind of dances a little faster. At one time or another, everyone at the rink takes notice of him.

Jobbi does two good things that I notice. First, he's way too quick on his skates for the other players to knock down — and believe me — most of them try. Second, he somehow scores two goals during the end of practice scrimmage — one goal into an open net on a rebound, and he scores the other by redirecting a shot along the ice. On that one, when Jobbi touches the puck with his stick, it completely changes course and the goalie is suddenly going the wrong way and can't recover in time to stop it. The shot that Jobbi redirects is taken by — of course — Pinger. Those are the only times during the whole scrimmage that I see Jobbi touch the puck. He's in and out of the front of the goal so fast that the other players don't seem to know who scored. After Jobbi's second goal, Jesse skates over to him and tries to congratulate him by giving him a pat on the top of the helmet, but Jobbi doesn't understand his intention and does this strange ducking, twisting, body-contorting escape that makes everyone laugh — except me. I know why he does that . . . when you're always dodging rocks, you learn to get out of the way first, then look for who's doing the throwing later.

I'm waiting for Jobbi outside the dressing room after practice. I hear the coach tell him that they've had a good look at him, but, unfortunately, they already have enough players and they have to cut him. Jobbi thanks him — a little too enthusiastically if you ask me. He puts all of the equipment Jesse loaned him back into the bag, and Jesse nods a thank you to him. Jobbi is the happiest guy in the world when we walk home. I think he's pleasantly surprised to still be alive. He's even happy to talk about girls with me, although he won't approve of any that I mention as possible girlfriends.

Jobbi's strategy of trying out for the hockey team to get the bullies off him ends up working — partially. He isn't generally harassed as much as he had been earlier. However, he's more harassed than ever by Wally, who greets Jobbi at school the next day with calls of what a loser he was to be cut from the team, and how he skated like a wiener and should wear a skirt when he's on the ice. He finishes by dubbing Jobbi 'Jobeena,' a name he obviously feels has some sort of figure-skating connection, but actually doesn't make any sense at all. Because of the brutal daily attacks by Wally, Jobbi hardly notices his newfound general acceptance.

As If

Paula

When I got home from school the day of the fight with my mom, I went straight upstairs and looked at myself in my mother's full-length mirror. I saw for the first time what a good job I'd done fitting in. I'd become so invisible that I couldn't see even a small piece of my real self anywhere in my reflection. I thought about Cheryl and began to understand her. She didn't need or care to fit in. She didn't have the time to worry about what some immature friends thought about her. Why did I? I was in grade eight now, not grade five. All the worry about pleasing people who weren't even my friends suddenly seemed so pointless. Who was I being invisible for anyway? It was for all the girls who made the rules about fitting in, which included me I suppose. I'd definitely followed those rules well enough. I wondered what would happen if I broke the code of remaining invisible? And did I really even care anymore?

I decided that it was time for a change — a big one. As far as how the other girls would take it, I was sure that I could handle whatever — just like Cheryl. It was time for me to find out if anyone could ever be interested in me in any serious way.

Thanksgiving weekend was coming up and we had Friday off too as a school administration day. I started my changeover by getting the colour out of my hair. I'd read that the veggie dye would come out faster if I shampooed with diet Sprite. By Saturday, I'd gone through four two-litre bottles and had pretty well got my hair back to its natural brown.

I needed a new hairstyle. My mom and I had made up the way we always did, by pretending our fight had never happened. She was surprisingly happy to spend ninety dollars for a haircut at *Hans for Hair.* It was sort of a Liv Tyler style — you know — with my hair down over one side of my face.

On Tuesday morning, I dawdled in the bathroom until I heard both parents leave for work. I put on eyeliner, lipstick, the tightest faded jeans I could get into, a pair of short-top, calf leather boots with spike heels that I'd found at our neighbour's garage sale, and a nice, tight-fitting, green-knit sweater that I'd picked up at the mall. It was a v-neck style, which I wore with a push-up bra. I wrapped a cute silver-studded belt around my waist that made the sweater fit perfectly. I wanted to let anyone know who cared to look, that I wasn't a shapeless little kid anymore.

Not

1142 Hillcrest Avenue

When Jobbi went to school, his mother tried to help with cleaning the house or cooking dinner, but it didn't work very well. Victor's mother had her own special ways. Taska understood that.

Taska eventually decided to look for a job, but her English, not being as good as Jobbi's, was a serious problem. Yet somehow or other, she found a Latvian woman who'd immigrated twenty-four years earlier and now ran a house-cleaning service. The woman gave Taska a try. Within a month, Taska became her most reliable worker, often working six full days a week. As the months passed, Taska was happy to use her earnings to contribute food and money for the extra expenses she and Jobbi caused their hosts.

During that same time in Latvia, things continued to be difficult for Taska's husband, Taylus. He couldn't afford a lawyer, and the government, likely because of the influence of Aija's father, wouldn't provide him with any legal help. That meant that he would have to defend himself in court. The charges brought against him were theft and conspiracy to commit fraud. The penalty, if he was found guilty, was up to four years in prison. The police claimed that he was involved in the plot to betray Aija Jumikis and steal the money and goods presented by the guests at her wedding. Of course, Taylus knew there was no such plot and was completely innocent. That knowledge made him feel certain that he would have no problem defending himself. What Taylus did not tell his family on the telephone was that the police questioned him often on the whereabouts of his wife. They obviously believed that she was also involved and might even have disappeared with the Russian, Boris Michalenkov. Taylus refused to tell them anything about Taska or Jobbi. All the police would say on those occasions was, "Hey. Fine. It will be your head."

The courts in Latvia, as in many countries, are crowded and slow to progress. Time and time again, Taylus' court dates were cancelled. Sometimes he would be informed beforehand about the cancellation, but most often not until he arrived at the courthouse. Finally, after many, many delays his case was called into the courtroom. Unfortunately, he wasn't present.

Only the day before his case was called into court, Taylus had found work as a parcel delivery driver for UPS. It was a good job with good pay, and because it was only his second day of work, he didn't want to ask for the time off to attend court. Instead, he had taken the chance that his court date would once again be cancelled. When the judge saw that Taylus was not present in the court, he ordered him arrested and locked in jail to ensure that he would be available for his next day in court, whenever that might happen.

When Taska learned of her husband going to jail, she immediately made up her mind to return to Latvia so she could be close to him, even though she would be risking jail herself.

There was no way that Jobbi could return with Taska to Valmiera, even though it was already May and there was only a month remaining in the school year. If both his mother and father ended up in jail, Latvian law would consider Jobbi an orphan and therefore property of the state. It would be unbearable for Taska and Taylus to lose their Jobbus, so they decided it would be safest for him to stay behind in Canada with his uncle, aunt and cousins until all of the misunderstandings were cleared up. He was thirteen years old by that time and understood the situation. Jobbi desperately wanted to return to help his father, but he agreed to stay behind as his mother requested.

On the day Taska left, everyone else was at work, leaving only Jobbi to say goodbye. Looking through the back window of the taxi toward the forlorn figure of her only son slowly disappearing, she felt as though her heart might completely break.

Whatever

Paula

I'll never forget that first day of school wearing my new look. It felt like my whole life changed, *snap*, just like that. I don't think I'm exaggerating much when I say that every boy in the school was checking me out. Even guys from the high school side went out of their way to say hi to me. Three boys in my grade started joking around with me every time they saw me. They'd never done that before. I don't think they'd even noticed me before. One of my worries was about how the teachers would react, but they were mostly just surprised and didn't say anything, not at first anyway.

It didn't take me long to decide that I liked the attention. Long before the bell rang at the end of the day, I'd already decided that this look was going to be me forever. Because, without anyone actually telling me, I felt beautiful. I'd taken a huge chance, but it had paid off. It was pretty clear to me that most guys liked what they saw.

And it wasn't just the guys who were impressed by my new look. The girls in my grade noticed too. No one teased me at first and when someone finally tried, I ignored it, exactly like Cheryl did. In the days that followed, things only got better and better for me. Every time I went into the girls' bathroom, someone would tell me how much they liked my style and how they'd like to change something of themselves — their hair, clothes, shoes, makeup — whatever. They wanted to know what I thought, like I was some kind of expert. I know that most of them really did want to do something too, but they also knew their parents would never let them.

My plan for dealing with my home was to keep this new, exciting life a secret for as long as possible. As I saw it, nothing good could come from my mom, stepdad or stepbrother seeing what I was up to.

As far as the teachers went, once they realized I was here to stay, they finally reacted. Twice I was called to the office and lectured by the vice-principal about dressing *appropriately* for school. The second time he actually told me I shouldn't wear clothes that draw attention to myself. I said, "But that's the whole point, isn't it?"

At the time, I was wearing these jeans that had a tear in the back and a small bit of my butt showed through. The VP sent me home to change, and by the time I got there, a school counsellor had already left a message for my parents. I erased it before they could get it. Unfortunately, I also erased another message, for my stepdad, about a client of his agreeing to some changes to some contract. He got pretty upset later about not getting that one.

As the days went on, my popularity continued to grow — among the boys; but I started to notice I was making my girlfriends feel deserted when I was around. I tried my best to include them, but the guys, especially the ones from the high school, didn't seem interested. Slowly but surely, I found myself walking the halls without any girlfriends around. Even Cheryl asked me, "What the hell's going on with you?"

It wasn't a friendly question. It was as though she felt I was intruding on her territory or something, which I obviously wasn't, not intentionally. She clearly didn't realize what an influence she'd had on me.

About a month after I changed, this particular guy I'd always liked, saw me coming into the lunchroom and made room for me at his table. I ended up being the only girl eating lunch with four of the coolest guys in the school. I don't quite know why, but that event seemed to be the last straw for most of my girlfriends. They all stopped talking to me completely, even my closest friends. And if they'd only stopped talking to me, that wouldn't have been so bad. It was the ones who went from being my friends all the way to hating me — that was really hard to take. Whatever. The truth was that if most of those girls were in my position, they'd feel exactly the same way I do.

My friends or former friends weren't my only problems. There was this group of girls who were considered to be a gang and who'd all been pretty popular before I *showed up.* For some reason they were particularly infuriated with me and started calling me names like slut, boy-toy, bitch, ho — all the regular stuff bullies say to bring you down. I ignored them at first, but one girl in the gang, who was the leader and pretty strong, started to 'accidentally' bump into me when we passed each other in the hallway. She eventually started pushing me into the lockers and even into other people when she got the chance. She was pretty sneaky about it. When I avoided her, she started having one of her gang members distract me while she came up from behind and knocked whatever I was carrying out of my arms.

One time, two high-school guys happened to be passing just as Colleen, the gang's leader, pulled that trick. They both stopped and helped me pick up my stuff. They'd seen what happened and one of them asked me what was wrong with that "little bitch," looking toward Colleen. I made a joke, saying she obviously liked me and was trying to get my attention. They laughed out loud, which I'm sure Colleen and her gang heard and recognized as being at their expense. The two guys hung around talking until they had to actually run to their class. The next day, one of my former friends warned me that the 'Dixie Roaders' — named for where the gang lived — were planning to beat the crap out of me and that I'd better not get caught alone with them.

It all got crazy so fast. On one side, I had all these guys who really couldn't seem to get enough of me, and on the other, these girls who used to be my friends; but now, not only did they not want anything to do with me, some of them were out to get me.

Whatever. They didn't scare me. For the first time in a long time I could see myself clearly, and I liked what I saw. The boys at our school obviously agreed, and that made me feel really good. There was no way I was giving any of that up just because some jealous, immature girls didn't like it.

You've Got To Be Kidding

Kevin

Jobbi is standing at a urinal, doing his business. The toilet cubicles are directly behind him. I'm washing my hands. I hear one of the cubicle doors open and see Wally Shumzicky come out right behind Jobbi, and before I can warn him, Wally grabs the back of Jobbi's pants and pulls him back away from the urinal. Jobbi lets out his usual squeal. "Aakveyaya! Leeksmimira!" — which is beginning to sound more and more like it might be a swear word in Latvian. Jobbi can't help spraying all over the place, including on his own shoes. Wally starts laughing in that kind of laugh that bullies use when they want everyone around to know that they've made a fool of somebody.

Jobbi doesn't have to turn around to know who's behind him. He zips up his pants, checks himself over, then turns around, and right in the middle of one of Wally's loud, attention-getting laughs, Jobbi pushes him hard in the chest with both hands. Wally isn't expecting that and stumbles backwards through the cubicle door all the way to the toilet, which he falls back into, rear end first. With the seat still up and Wally being so small, he sinks right down into the bottom of the bowl, which hasn't been flushed. He gets himself out fast, but not without a lot of splashing, and not before the back of his jeans are completely soaked with the filthy yellow water. Wally starts to say something to Jobbi like, 'You're in trouble now,' but Jobbi cuts him off. I can't believe it when he says, "Vally, chyou learrrn tew flosh, hokay?" I laugh out loud and have a hard time stopping when Wally gives me a look to warn me that I'll be in for the same when it comes to him getting his revenge. He checks himself in the mirror and almost starts to cry, then leaves quickly — to go home and change, I suspect. After Wally takes off, Jobbi smiles and gives me a high five.

Obviously

Stephanie

Kevin called me and told me about Jobbi pushing Wally into the toilet. I was shocked, but happy to hear what had happened. We both agree that Pinger will totally be coming after Jobbi and we decide that we should try to help Jobbi stay clear of him. But the next morning, as I'm walking in through the northwest entrance of the school, Pinger pushes past me and charges down the hallway, straight to the junior-high lockers. Everyone knows what's going down and there's already a small crowd following him. I try my best to get past and warn Jobbi, but there's no way. I'm so hoping that Jobbi is making himself scarce, but to everyone's surprise he isn't hiding at all. He's just squatting at his locker sorting out his books for the morning classes.

Pinger marches up behind him, grabs Jobbi by the shirt collar and spins him around! Jobbi doesn't even have time to stand up or let go of the books he's holding. Pinger's arm is pulled back and ready to punch Jobbi in the face. Suddenly, a loud voice calls from down the hall. It's Pinger's good buddy/follower/teammate, Basil Kamali.

"Ping! Hold on a sec."

Pinger looks at Bas without letting go of Jobbi or unclenching his fist. Jobbi is dangling by his collar and looking up at Pinger all defiant-like. Bas pushes through the crowd, then whispers something to Pinger and stands back to watch Pinger's reaction.

"What! This little shit? You've got to be kidding?"

Bas shrugs like he's just as shocked about the information he just passed on. Pinger so can't believe it and now seems even more pissed, but instead of punching Jobbi, he lets go of him with a shove and sends Jobbi and his books skidding across the floor.

"You are so lucky, Newbie." Pinger is sneering. "And you better keep your hands off of my little brother and quit picking on him all the time . . . I don't care if we are teammates . . . I'll kick the crap out of you. You understand that, Newbie?"

Suddenly, Jobbi scrambles up off the floor. Instead of collecting his books, he charges right at Pinger. I can tell he's mad and ready to fight no matter what. Pinger isn't expecting that from Jobbi and takes a couple of quick steps back in surprise, ducking his head behind his raised hands to protect himself. Just then, this giant body steps out from the crowd around them and puts himself right between Jobbi and Pinger. It's Mr. Dixon!

"Talking a little hockey here, are we boys?"

I'm the one who tipped off Jesse to bring Jobbi some hockey equipment for that practice. After school that day, I see Jesse walking into the 7-Eleven and I get off the bus to talk to him. It isn't Jobbi I want to talk about, but his name comes up, and after I tell him how Jobbi wants to try out for the team, but doesn't have the equipment, Jesse does the rest.

I also tell him about how bad things are in our end of the school this year and he says he knows all about it. I want to know if he has any ideas for something that could be done. He says he doesn't know for sure, but he knows someone I might ask. It turns out that the hallway protest he led last year to get the principal to allow the fall dance? That wasn't all his idea. There was a teacher he'd talked to — about that and a few other things too. He asks me if I'd tried to talk to her yet.

"No. I so have no idea who you're talking about. And why would I talk to her anyway?"

"Well, the truth is that if you want things to be different, Stephanie, then you're the one who has to do it. That's just the way it is."

"But I'm no — I mean I can't . . . you know."

"All the same, you should talk to Dufault."

"Old lady Dufault? Who teaches Immersion Geography?"

"Yep. And she's really not that old. But she won't talk to you when the other teachers are around. You have to catch her when she's alone."

I follow Jesse's suggestion and two days later at 4:30 pm, I get together with Ms. Dufault in her classroom. She seems pretty suspicious of me and acts like she has no idea what I'm talking about when I mention the crazy state I think the school is in. That forces me to tell her that Jesse had suggested I talk to her. She sighs, and looks at me like I'm the last sloppy-joe on the hot food tray in the cafeteria — and she isn't sure she has the stomach for it.

I completely understand. I'm almost a nobody when it comes to school popularity. I think she was expecting some kid who, with the right advice from her, could go and get things done — someone like Jesse, who only has to walk down the hall and everyone follows. Dufault obviously trusts him. The truth is there aren't that many kids who even know my last name. I try to reassure her.

"I know that I can't do much on my own, but things are so bad around here, I feel like somebody's gotta try. And I do have some friends who can help." I even surprise myself saying that — the friends part, that is. I realize for the first time that I'm not talking about Rena or Jenny or Gail. It's Kevin and Jobbi I have in mind.

Ms. Dufault obviously decides that I don't have whatever she thought it took and that I'm too risky to take a chance on.

"Well, I suppose you must do what you feel you can do, Stephanie. You are certainly free to try. However, if you'd like a word of personal advice?"

Finally. I give her my full attention.

"Don't take on more than you can handle, Ms. Horner. That won't help anyone."

Great. Thanks a lot.

Why doesn't she just say she thinks I'm too stupid or useless to be getting involved in such serious matters? Her words hurt. Even the ones she doesn't say. It should be plenty enough *encouragement* for me to give up, except for one thing. I know my mother and sister would have had the same evaluation of me. They all consider me a lightweight with little or no chance of ever being able to make any kind of difference to anyone. Whatever.

It's a lot harder to give up when you find yourself in front of an audience.

I'll do it without their help.

Whatever

1142 Hillcrest Ave.

Jobbi worked hard at learning English and by the time the next school year started, grade eight for him, he was pretty good at it, but still found it difficult to speak to anyone except those who were close. He also delivered ninety-two newspapers for *The Sun* every morning before school. He gave the money he earned to his uncle to help with his living expenses. His mother called every Sunday for the first couple of months she was away. Then money for long distance phone calls became scarce for her and she was only able to call once a month. Jobbi's aunt also called Taska once a month, mostly for his sake.

Unfortunately, things were not going too well in Latvia. After several months and many threats by the police, Taska was able to negotiate an agreement with them. The prosecutor told Taska that she and Taylus would not be prosecuted for theft or conspiracy to commit fraud as long as Taska brought them Boris Michalenkov, or whatever his real name was. Taska had no idea where or how to find him, but she promised that she would do whatever she had to do in order to clear her husband and herself. The Prosecutor gave her three months. In the meantime, Taylus would be remaining in custody.

Taska found a hairdressing job to support herself while she figured out how to find Michalenkov. The shop was in Valka, a city right on the border with Estonia and about forty kilometres from Valmiera. She went there because she knew that she could not endure the suspicion or mistrust of her former clients and co-workers at her old salon. She worked hard all day in Valka, then spent every possible spare hour trying to find the man who had ruined their lives.

Jobbi suspected that things weren't going well in Latvia. Even though his mother never said anything about her troubles when they spoke, there was no happiness in her voice. As for Jobbi, he definitely didn't want his mother to worry about him. They spoke only Latvian during their calls. Jobbi's enthusiastic descriptions of his many friends and the fun he was having at his new school was an exaggeration intended to give his mother peace of mind.

The actual truth was that he was not sure he could stay in school much longer. He had promised both his parents that he would work hard and succeed so they could all, someday, be together again and have a happy life. But almost everything in Canada was difficult for him. He felt sick thinking about school every morning when he got up to deliver his papers. The weather had turned cold and wet in November and his thin jacket did not keep him warm or dry. His aunt and uncle tried to protect him, but they could not do much about the things that happened while they were at work, which was most of the time.

Jobbi was lonely in his basement room, especially when Victor was away at university. His English speaking had improved, but reading and writing it was slow, and he received low marks in some courses because he was not able to complete the tests in the required time. Only in math and computer science was he able to keep up and do well. The teachers were encouraging, yet they seemed completely powerless to stop the bullying he suffered.

The one thing that gave Jobbi hope was his friend, Kevin, and a new friend — a girl named Stephanie. They were talking and spending more time together.

Then, unexpectedly, at the beginning of December, in his second year at Central, things began to change.

You Wish

Kevin

As far as I know, there isn't a real geek club in school *per se*. There isn't an official membership card or president or any list of who is and isn't in the club either, but they recognize one another. Geeks are easy to spot — especially when you're mistaken for one as much as I am. For the most part they've learned to accept who they are and try not to get too hurt, physically or the other way — you know, feelingswise.

When Jobbi jumped up off the floor today and wanted to fight Pinger, I could feel the hair on my arms stand up. He didn't care that he would have gotten the worst of it; he'd had enough and wasn't going to take anymore. And it was Pinger who stepped back to protect himself. For my friends and me, it was like watching some kind of geek super hero. As far as we're concerned, it's a massive victory. In one moment, Jobbi goes from being the school's favourite bully target to King of the Central School Geek Nation. And I'm his best friend, his only friend. Well, there's Stephanie, but . . . I don't know. Anyway, all morning — all day in fact — the whole geek crowd in our section of the school has been walking taller. They're nodding and smiling to one another in the hallway, high-fiving awkwardly for no reason, and answering questions in class without worrying about how they look or whether the other kids think they're cool.

As usual, Jobbi doesn't have a clue what he's done or what the heck is going on. I stay close to him, though, and take it all in for both of us. It's like I'm his right hand man and everyone wants to say hi to him through me. If he notices all the kids watching him while he eats lunch, he doesn't let on. He's pretty cool really.

In my position as official Number One to the Big Guy, I decide to work the room at lunchtime, just in case there is going to be some trouble with Wally or Pinger in the toilets after we finish eating. That's where it's going to happen if anything will. Devon, Colin and Murray all say they'll be there for back-up if Jobbi needs them.

After eating, we bunch together and follow him. I have butterflies in my stomach and Colin's eyes are almost bugging out of his head. Jobbi must sense that something is up, because before we can follow him through the washroom door, he turns and holds up his hand like a stop sign. We all mill around outside, waiting until he comes out. Devon is almost pulling the seams off his pants, he's so nervous. When the door opens, it isn't Jobbi who steps out. It's Wally. Everyone freezes. Wally looks at us and says something under his breath that we can barely hear. It sounds like "Freepin greek skod." We look at one another, slightly confused, as he walks away. I don't know where Murray gets it, but he yells out, "Hope you didn't have another accident?" A couple of us laugh. Then we remember that Jobbi is still inside and rush for the door. He steps out first, still in one piece. There's a single huge — and I mean huge — sigh of relief from all of us. We walk down the main hallway together, heading back to class feeling pretty good about ourselves.

Not

Paula

I started coming home after school via the back lane and through the garage. I kept an oversized, button-up sweater inside a cardboard box there. I put it on to cover up whatever I was wearing until I could get into my room and change. I also hid my stiletto boots out there. As for around the house, I'd wear the biggest, sloppiest sweats that I could find. Even so, I could still feel my stepbrother's eyes on me whenever he was around. I didn't like that, so I tried to avoid him as much as possible, which is hard when you live together.

Most of the time, there was no one home after school, although, once in a while Dylan would be there. This one day when I got home from school I didn't see Dylan's bike in the yard, so I left the big sweater in the garage. As I walked past a room my parents used for an office, Dylan suddenly jumped out and wrapped his arms around me from behind, pinning my arms to my side. He was surprisingly strong. I kind of yelled playfully, hoping that he was only joking. I asked him to let me go. Instead, he put his face in my ear and whispered, "I've been watching you. I know what you're up to."

His breath smelled horrible. Like he'd been drinking. I decided to get angry instead of how I really felt — scared out of my mind. "LET GO OF ME DYLAN — RIGHT NOW!"

Instead of letting me go, I felt him tighten his grip. It got hard to breathe. Was this what being squeezed by a python felt like? That's when the phone rang. For a second I didn't think that he'd let me go to answer it. Then his dad's voice came on over the answering message. "Dylan or Paula. If you're there, pick up." Dylan finally let go of me and answered. I ran upstairs to my room as fast as I could and locked the door. My heart was pounding out of my chest and my legs were shaking. I had no idea what I could do if he came after me again. But the next thing I heard from downstairs was the front door closing as Dylan left the house. I watched him from my window until he disappeared down the street.

I didn't tell my mom or anyone about what had happened. I knew she was having her own problems. As for my real dad, I was seeing him less and less. The last time was on my birthday, four months earlier. He's a transport truck driver and hardly ever home. That was one of the big problems for my mom when they were married.

Dylan didn't come back for a couple of days. I'm sure he thought that I'd told his dad what had happened. The night he returned, I heard his old man yelling and knocking him around down in his room. Later, my mom told me that Dylan had come home drunk and his dad had also discovered that he'd been stealing bottles of booze from the house.

After that night, Dylan made a point of ignoring me whenever we were in the same room. Still, I could tell he'd figured out that I hadn't said anything to our parents about him threatening me — not yet anyway. Despite that, twice now I thought someone lifted an extension while I was on the phone. And the other night, something woke me. I'm almost certain there was someone standing outside my room. As worried as I was about my life at home before, I was even more worried now.

Yeah, Right

Stephanie

Vice-Principal Wickens almost jumps out of his office chair when I give him my plan about having a dance. I can see right away that he agrees with me that a dance might be a way to turn around all the bad stuff that is going on in the school. But then, he has second thoughts about it. His face changes, and I know he's considering the other possibilities. It's true — a dance could also end up being a disaster and make things even worse. And going by what I'd heard from Jesse, I guess Mr. Wickens could even end up getting in some trouble himself.

I try to convince Mr. Wickens that my idea will work without really telling him what I have planned. I guarantee him that everyone in the junior high section of the school will come, and that it'll be a lot of fun, and that there'll be plenty of supervision to make sure everything goes ok. He stares at me for a few seconds, then he asks, "Who?"

I'm surprised he asks, but try to sound confident saying that I've already spoken to several teachers who are ready to help out, and all I need is a date and time so they can confirm that they'll be available. He tells me that if I can convince six teachers and six parents to act as supervisors, then he will talk to the principal about approving a dance for the last Thursday night before the start of the Christmas break. Wow! That's only sixteen days away. Sixteen days to get everything ready. First, I have to have all the names of the teachers and parents willing to supervise the dance on his desk by Friday noon. It's Tuesday.

The first three teachers I talk to about supervising the dance say that they'd love to help, but are too busy doing their own Christmas-type stuff. Not good. It's pretty easy to see that's what everyone will say when I ask, even the parents.

Later that day, I come across Ms. Dufault in the hallway. She stops to talk to me. My guess is that she's feeling a little guilty about not helping me. She asks me how things are going and I wonder if she really cares, but since I don't have much to lose anyway I tell her about what's going on. She rolls her eyes and gives me this tired little smile, then asks, "Stephanie. When teachers were your age, what sort of students do you suppose they were?"

"I don't know. Like me, I guess?"

"A few perhaps, but no, not most. Think again."

"Well, they were probably good students . . . "

"How good? Hmm?"

She looks at me as though it's some secret that she's sworn on a stack of dictionaries never to reveal, but one that I should be able to figure out on my own — if I had any brains at all that is. That was so no help.

"You can put my name down on your list if you like." Huh?! That takes me by surprise. Then, as she's walking away, she adds over her shoulder. "Let me know if your dance gets cancelled — so I can plan to do something else."

Though the teachers are a problem, the parents, surprisingly, aren't. I have more than six of them lined up in one evening of phone calls. Okay. That makes me feel so better and keeps me from throwing in the towel, which I hate to admit, I could easily do. I continue to work on my plan in my head. One of the many problems is how to get all of the geeks to take a chance and show up. They never want to show up to anything because they always end up getting picked on. To start with, I know I shouldn't call them geeks. Probably *socially challenged* is better — or maybe even better: so'challs. It's an important part of my plan to make sure that everyone in the school will be there. It's critical. Suddenly it hits me — what Dufault was saying: teachers were geeks! Socially challenged! When our teachers were in junior high, they were probably the socially challenged kids of their schools.

The next day I decide to hit on the teachers who still seem a little socially challenged. I tell them how I'm trying to organize a dance that is about bringing kids together — the cool kids, the shy kids, the jocks, the metal heads, the hippies, and especially the geeks. I tell them that the purpose of the dance is to make sure that everyone will have fun and get a chance to meet guys (if it's a female teacher) or girls (for the males).

My strategy works crazy good! I can actually see the teachers I approach thinking back to their own junior high school days and remembering how painful it had been for them. Then I say, "Take a guy like Jobbi. Without a dance, he doesn't stand a chance of ever meeting a girl. He'll be all alone for, like, ever!" I know it's kind of Degrassie-ish, but for some reason they all see a little bit of themselves in him. One after another they sign on the dotted line.

I put the names in on Thursday and the dance is approved the next day. Now all I have to do is live up to all the promises I've made to Mr. Wickens.

Get A Clue

Kevin

I have no idea why Jobbi was asked back to the hockey team. Jobbi doesn't seem to know either. Word of it got around the school though, and by the time he and I find Jesse on the high-school side of the school, Jobbi doesn't even have to ask — Jesse is way ahead of him. "Don't worry, I'll bring the equipment. Just make sure you show up with your goal-scoring stick."

I can see Jobbi wondering what a goal-scoring stick is. As far as he knows, he only has *one* hockey stick. I tell him what Jesse meant. Jobbi still doesn't seem to get it. Then, later that day, he finds a small roll of black stick tape hanging by the sticky end to the door of his locker. He looks at me to explain what it's all about.

"I don't know why it's there . . . unless . . . do you have any of this on your stick? Do you have any tape on your hockey stick, Jobbi? I don't think you do."

I explain to Jobbi that the blade of his stick should be taped so the puck doesn't slide off it so easily, and that the shaft of the stick should also be taped so that his top hand will have a better grip to hold on to. Jobbi tells me that, in Latvia, he used some heavy tape to keep his old stick from falling apart. His new stick isn't falling apart, though. In fact, it barely has a mark on it. He actually used a cloth to rub off the one puck mark it did get.

I'm not a big hockey fan, but I have to admit that going to tryouts and practices with Jobbi has been pretty interesting so far. That night, Mr. Bauer gets me to help him pass out the practice jerseys. He has a list that one of the coaches gave him. As I'm looking through the box for numbers, I see a player — a big grade-niner by the name of Kris Cerps — walking across the dressing room, and without saying anything, he grabs Jobbi's stick. I can see that Jobbi isn't sure how to handle this guy helping himself to his stuff. The guy checks the stick over and then measures it against his own height by standing the stick on its toe in front of him. Then he says, "First of all, it's too long for you. You should probably cut off at least five centimetres. And this . . . " He points to the blade, shaking his head. "This is, like, the worst tape job, maybe ever."

All the other players in the room chuckle. Jobbi is watching Kris carefully to see if he intends to damage the only stick he owns. Kris makes this big sigh, then starts to peel off the tape that Jobbi had put on earlier. Jobbi jumps up and tries to take his stick back, but Kris, who's huge, just kind of turns his back to him and continues tearing off the tape. It only takes him a few seconds, even while he's holding Jobbi off. When all the tape is off, Kris turns to Jobbi and starts snapping his fingers impatiently. I can see that Jobbi finally gets the idea that this guy is trying to show him something, and needs his roll of tape to do it. Jobbi digs the roll out of his jacket pocket and hands it to Kris, who peels off about a forty-centimetre-long strip and holds it up for him to see.

"You take a piece this long and twist it at both ends about eight or ten times — until it looks like a rope. Got it? You wrap the rope around the shaft, nice and tight, about roughly where the fingers of your top hand grip the stick. Now you take the tape roll and cover that rope like a blanket. Make it nice and tight too, all the way down to the bottom of your grip so nothing will come loose during the game. Make sure that the butt end is covered too. It's a penalty if it isn't covered during a game because it can easily injure another player. Put a couple of extra strips over the end, just in case."

As he finishes with the handle of the stick, Kris tears the tape with his teeth, then quickly flips the stick around and shows Jobbi how to do the two-direction, opposite-side method of taping the blade. He finishes the job with the tape strip near the heel of the blade. Then he uses the edge of a puck to smooth out the rough spots. All in all, it takes Kris less than five minutes to tape both ends. When he's done, he hands the stick back to Jobbi and flips him what's left of the tape roll. Jobbi checks out his stick. It's a perfect tape job, just like all of the other guys' sticks. Jobbi is pretty happy with it.

I don't see the first part of the practice because me and Mr. Bauer are getting blood stains from the previous year off some of the game jerseys. He has this neat trick of using an eye-dropper with water, some table salt and an old toothbrush. There are quite a few stains. Mr. Bauer isn't a guy who talks a lot except when he's explaining something, and even then he lets me figure out stuff for myself.

While we're working in this empty dressing room we hear one of the assistant coaches talking to Jesse's dad out in the hall. They're talking about three of the team's best players and biggest goal scorers, whose parents took them off the team because Principal Largebutt made this new rule that all players had to have a sixty-five per cent subject average to play. If anyone falls below that they'll be suspended until their marks improve. The three players had switched over to a community team so they wouldn't miss any time playing. Jesse's dad and the coach just start talking about how upset Coach West was and how losing those players meant total disaster for the team this year, when Mr. Bauer clears his throat to let them know that we can hear them. So they move away. That explains why Jobbi got on the team, though.

When I get out to watch the practice, I notice right away that it doesn't look like the other players are looking for a chance to get Jobbi like before. It's almost as though they don't mind that he's there.

I'd have to say, from what I see out on the ice that Jobbi's not doing too good. He tries hard, but all of the skating drills are fast and difficult. He definitely isn't used to all the bulky equipment he's wearing. The puck drills are even harder for him, although his stick does catch and hold on to the puck much more easily than when he didn't have any tape on it.

Mr. Bauer said he'd come and find me if I he needs me again, so I climb up into the stands. Some grade-nine girls I know are there watching the practice. They notice Jobbi but don't know who he is. I tell them a little bit about him. "He skates kinda funny," pretty much sums up their impression of him.

After a lot of non-stop skating drills, all of the players line up at centre ice, and a coach passes them a puck, one at a time. The player then skates in on the goalie to try to score. Jobbi looks nervous waiting for his turn. When he gets to the front of the line, coach Dixon passes him a puck across the ice. When the puck hits his stick, it flies right out of his hands. Then, when he tries to pick the stick up off the ice, he can't because of the thick fingers on his hockey gloves. It's actually kind of comical watching — from where I am anyway.

The next player in line, and the one after that, both have their turns before Jobbi finally gets his stick and the puck back. But instead of going back to the end of the line and waiting for another turn, Jobbi takes off straight for the goal. He is coming from an angle and doesn't notice that the goalie is looking at the next shooter in line, and not at him. When Jobbi is around five meters away, he shoots the puck as hard as he can. It sails way wide of the net, and the effort of it knocks him first off one skate, then the other. He falls to the ice, but his momentum carries him straight into Mitch Chung, the goalie. At the very last second, Mitch sees Jobbi coming. He jumps as high as he can, hoping that Jobbi will pass underneath him. It doesn't work. Jobbi's elbow catches the bottom of Mitch's skate, spins the goalie around in the air and lands him on the ice head-first.

Jobbi ends up inside the goal with his skates tangled in the mesh. When Mitch gets back on his skates, he can't continue the practice. He injured his neck. Mitch's girlfriend — who I've been talking to — slugs me in the shoulder really hard . . . "Give that to your stupid friend for me," she says.

There's only one goalie, the backup, left for the scrimmage game at the end of practice. Jobbi doesn't touch the puck the whole time. The dressing room definitely isn't as friendly as it had been before practice.

Sure

1142 Hillcrest Ave.

Victor watched as Jobbi carried his large, heavy hockey bag down the stairs to the basement. Jobbi didn't see him sitting in the dark. As Jobbi began to hang up his wet equipment, he noticed the voices of his aunt and uncle arguing upstairs. It sounded strange to him because, normally, they didn't raise their voices much. His uncle was angry about something and it was just as clear that his aunt was not giving in on whatever the argument was about. They were speaking Latvian, and Jobbi just began to realize that, when Victor's voice startled him.

"You are playing hockey?"

"Aakveyaya!"

Victor turned on the lamp beside his chair so Jobbi could see him — and his bottle of rye. Victor was supposed to be at university until Christmas break, so he was pretty sure that Jobbi knew something wasn't right.

"It is me they are yelling about. I dropped out of school. My dad is so pissed; he wants me to go to work at the shop with him tomorrow morning."

Victor takes a drink from his bottle and grunts as the liquid burns in his throat.

"My mom is saying that they should give me some time to figure things out. Ha. You know what is so funny? I do not even know how I know that. I can barely speak Latvian anymore. They are the only ones who ever speak it to me. I have been in Canada since I was five. I do not even remember *the wonderful* Valmiera or anything about Latvia. Hey. You wanna shot, Jobbi?"

He held the bottle out for Jobbi.

"It is rye. You should try it. The best thing ever to come out of Canada, including Wayne Gretzky."

Jobbi waved off the offer.

"Ah Veekturus. Hulloa. Ahyes, hi plays da hoakey forrr mwy skooill. Umm porrrahps."

"Oh! You are still in tryouts? I never tried out. They would not let me — my parents, that is. I had to learn accordion."

"Accorrrdioan. Hey! Me, hi tew pilays."

"Cool. So, hey. How are the tryouts goin'?"

"Ah goud, goud . . . Nah. Nah. Note so goud. Iss vahrrri harrrd tew . . ."

"Keep up and not get killed?"

"Ahyes. Note tew be keeled. Iss vahrrri harrrd. Hows arrr chyou, Veekturrrus?"

"Victor, Jobbi. Remember? Even better, Vic, not Victurus."

"Ahyes. Mmm sauhrrry Veekturr . . . Veek"

"Nah, nah. Do not apologize. Ah, it is me, Jobbi. I just could not stay there anymore. At university. I had to come home."

"Hmm. Bot, chyou dooz sooo werrry werrry goud at da yunvarrrceetay. Noa?"

"Yeah. I guess. If you only count school work, then yeah, I was doing pretty good."

"Hokay. Hokay. Hi see dis. Iss da bahd peopulls whoe pooshes chyou en paunch en hit fairrr no rrraisun, hey?"

"Bullies, you mean? Nah. It is not that. Hey, not unless the bully's name is — Brandi Shaw."

"Burondee? A garrrul? Garrrul heets chyou? . . . Evrrry day?"

"Nope. Not every day. Just one punch. Right in the stomach."

"Wass eet harrrd paunch . . . Veek?"

"Oh yeah. Hey. Real hard."

Vic closed his eyes and even though Jobbi waited patiently, they didn't open again. Jobbi threw a blanket over his cousin, then went to bed himself. But instead of dreaming about hockey, or bullies, or the growling Rottweiler on his paper route, he visited the Boris-Aija wedding night, the night that had changed his family's life so much.

That's Ridiculous

Paula

Last Saturday, I was on the number seventeen bus coming home from downtown, when the Dixie Road gang got on. They saw me right away and sat down all around me so that I couldn't get out of my seat. They started with calling me names, all of which I'd heard many times.

At some point, I realized that I didn't see where the big girl had gone. Before I could turn around and look for her, she slapped me on the side of the head from the seat behind me. I jumped up and managed to push her hard in the chest. When I did, the three other girls joined in by pulling my hair and hitting me with slaps and punches anywhere they could.

I fought back hard, mostly to get the attention of the bus driver. He finally stopped the bus and came back. The gang put on their poor-little-innocent-girls act, while I stayed tough to let them know I wasn't afraid of them. The driver did the easiest thing, which was to kick me off the bus.

While I was gathering my stuff, the big girl said to me quietly, "You're one dead bitch." Two of the other girls made faces at me in the back window as the bus drove away. Colleen pointed at me with one hand and ran a finger across her throat with the other.

There'd been a lot of other problems at school. Fights were happening almost every day. I heard one kid nearly lost an eye during a brawl in the boys' gym lockers. The teachers clearly couldn't protect everyone. I felt like I was on my own. That's why I grabbed the knife from the teacher's desk and put it in my bag. No one saw me.

Forget About It

Russia/Latvia Border

It was early December now and Taska's three months were almost up.

A woman customer of the salon told Taska a story. It seemed there was a Russian student from the University of Estonia who had jilted a young woman from Polva on their wedding night three years before. The cad had been followed by the poor girl's retired military uncle all the way to the North of Russia, somewhere north of St. Petersburg. Her uncle managed to learn that the man was already married with two children, but encountered only a stone wall of silence when he tried to get closer. The similarities to Aija's Boris seemed too close to ignore. When Taska took this news to the police in Valmiera and asked them to call their colleagues in St. Petersburg to investigate further, the policeman laughed at her.

"How do you know this for certain? Eh? And if it is true, do you think Russian police officers are interested in spending their time and money to arrest one of their own citizens, who managed to dupe a few Latvian saps? They would much prefer to find him so they could congratulate him on his cleverness, and maybe have a drink of vodka and some laughs together at our expense."

Taska was crushed. In total desperation, she decided to take the train to St. Petersburg herself — despite not having any clear plan of what she would do once she got there. The shop owner and friend where Taska worked in Valka, loaned her the money for the ticket. The owner hoped that Taska would eventually return to the shop, because the customers liked her and appreciated her work. The woman also knew of Taska's great burden and feared it would distract her from that work if it was ignored.

Taska had no idea how she would find Michalenkov — or whatever his name was — when she got to St. Petersburg. Her only chance was to trust that an opportunity would present itself along the way. She believed in her heart that this injustice would not be rewarded.

A further complication for Taska was that she had only a few days left to bring in Boris Michalenkov before her husband would go to trial.

When she was finally on the train to St. Petersburg, Taska couldn't help but think of her son so far away in Canada. Was he safe? Was he happy? Were her brother-in-law and sister-in-law protecting him? Were they making certain that he did not get ill, or lost, or heartsick? Was he making friends? Did her son know that his *mãmina* and his *tẽtuks* think about him all day, every day? Before she knew it, tears had come to her eyes. Just then, the train stopped. Taska looked out the window and recognized the Russian border customs stop. Soldiers were boarding the train to check the passengers' papers. She took her documents out of her bag.

"Documents, please?" It was a woman soldier with a big rifle hanging from her shoulder. She smiled at Taska, but quickly changed her expression when she saw the tears in Taska's eyes.

"So, what is this?"

The woman motioned toward Taska's tear-streaked face. As soon as Taska began to tell her the story of her husband's arrest, their son's exile in Canada, and her own desperation to get to St. Petersburg and find the Russian man who had caused it all, she began to cry, sob actually. Before she could tell the woman soldier about the guilt she felt, which only another woman could understand, the guard took a small radio from her belt, and in Russian, spoke the word "troublemaker" into it.

Taska was shocked. She tried harder, in her imperfect Russian, to explain her position to the woman, but moments later another guard arrived, a very large man. He asked Taska to come with him. She refused, instead grabbing the back of her seat with both hands. He took hold of her arms with his hands, wrenching her fingers from the seat and lifting her into the air. Taska fought by trying to wrap her legs around anything in the passenger car that she could reach, but the guard was too strong. She could see how much she frightened the other passengers when she cried out for help, but she felt she had no choice. The woman guard followed Taska off the train with her handbag and small satchel.

Taska was deposited on the platform and remained there, under guard, until the train departed without her. She had no strength left to fight. She stayed on the platform doing the only thing she could think of — praying, until dark.

Later that night the same woman guard, no longer wearing a uniform or carrying a rifle, returned to the station and got Taska onto her feet and into a Lada. The woman then drove back across the border to the town of Vilaka, Latvia, twenty kilometres away. She let Taska out at the bus station. The only words spoken between the women were, “Come. It is time to start your journey home.” “Will you be all right if I leave you here?” and “Thank you for your kindness.” The remainder of the sad journey was silent.

As If

Kevin

Me and Jobbi are being jostled along the school hallway, trapped in the river of students flowing between afternoon classes. Lately, I'm finding the crowded hallway a place I don't mind. Suddenly, hands grab the backs of both our shirts and pull us sideways into an emergency door alcove. Jobbi yelps.

"Aakveyaya! Leeksmimira!"

I think I call for my mom.

"Wow. Nervous much, you guys?"

It's Stephanie.

"Okay, I think I've got this dance so figured out."

I'm used to answering for Jobbi in situations like this, but before I can speak, he does. "Stayfoonie! Howu arrres chyou?"

Even Steph is a little surprised.

"Me? Oh. I'm fine. Thanks, Jobbi. Please listen to me, both of you."

With that, she quickly pokes both of us in the chest just above the heart using the tip of her left index finger — first me, then him. I can't believe the effect she has on Jobbi when she touches him. His eyes blink out for a second, and his body twitches like he's been zapped with an electrical charge. Steph is so focused on what she has to tell us that she doesn't seem to notice.

"Listen to me, you guys."

She pokes us in the chest again, and again Jobbi's eyes close, only this time he sort of smiles and leans against the door for support. I wonder if he's going to pass out. Steph is beginning to think that we're making fun of her. She shakes her head and decides to stop poking us, because it isn't getting her the kind of attention she wants.

"Kevin. Jobbi. The dance is in ten days, on the nineteenth. I could really use both of you to help me with it. Will you help me?"

"Sure, Steph, no problem. What do you want me to do?"

"Kevin, I need you to help make sure that everyone in the middle school comes to the dance. I'm personally inviting as many kids as I can get around to. It would really help if you could talk to all the socially challenged kids?"

"Huh? Social what?"

"Socially challenged? You know. The so'challs? She lowers her voice. "The geeks? I promised Vice-Principal Wickens I'd make sure that *everyone* would be there."

I'm more than a little put off. "Oh, sure. Right. I get it. I can do that because you think I'm one of them, right?"

Stephanie tilts her head to the side with this little smile on her face. It's that look that girls give you when they have to tell you something about yourself that you obviously don't realize.

"Kevin, you're the coolest geek in this school. And you're their hero. They'll totally come if you ask them."

I can't believe that Stephanie thinks of me as a geek. To be honest, though, it isn't a total shock. Everybody thinks I'm one. Stephanie is also my friend. A good friend. And I know she isn't saying it to hurt me. So what if, maybe, I am almost a geek. That's not that big a deal. Besides, it's also the first time anyone ever called me "cool."

"Okay, Steph. Since you put it that way. I'll give it a try."

"You so won't have any problem, Kevin. Trust me." She touches my shoulder in a reassuring way. "I could also use some help decorating the gym the day of the dance, and taking tickets at the door?"

"No prob. I'll be there. Next Thursday, right?" She nods and turns her attention to Jobbi, looking straight into his eyes. Her intense gaze is way more than his already spinning brain can handle. She might as well stick him in the heart with an electric cattle prod. I grab his arm with both hands because I'm worried he's going to pass out and end up on the floor. For some reason, Steph still doesn't notice how far away in lala-land he is. She starts to talk to him in her sweetest voice.

"I know you're, like, on the hockey team now, Jobbi, and you have to practice or play, like, almost every night. But I only need you to do one thing. Show up a bit early for the dance and work with me and Kevin at the door? The dance starts at eight o'clock, so if you could be here, say, around seven-thirty, that would be *purrrfect.* Will you? Please? Work with me at the door?"

She pauses — for emphasis, I think.

"It's very, very important that you say yes, Jobbi."

I can tell that Jobbi is trying his best to pull himself together. Obviously, he doesn't want to disappoint Steph. As for her, it's as though she can't imagine having the kind of effect on anyone that she is having on Jobbi. Again, I'm about to answer for him, when he surprises me.

"Hi, hi . . . hi vood lie-ik tew helps chyou . . . Stayfoonie." It almost sounds like he's slurring his words, although given the way he always talks, it's hard to tell for sure.

"You would? Really, Jobbi?" Steph was genuinely excited.

"Voood. Rrrailly-sh."

Okay, that is definitely slurred this time.

"That would be so excellent. Thank you." She pokes him again, but in a friendly way because now she knows he's enjoying it.

"Okay. Be here at seven-thirty next Thursday night." She takes a pad with big rings on it out of her book bag. There's a long list of items written on the top page. I can see my name and Jobbi's on the list beside "Door." She crosses us off, then looks directly into Jobbi's eyes again.

"Promise me?"

I'm barely able to hold him up so he can nod his head at her.

"Prrrom asa da."

Steph makes a happy sigh, then disappears into the flow of bodies. It's a few minutes before Jobbi can remember where he is and what he's supposed to be doing.

He's so gone on her.

You Wish

Paula

That day I took the knife, I fell asleep in my bedroom after I got home. When I woke up, it was dark and I heard someone coming down the hall toward my room. I had the knife under my pillow. The footsteps stopped right outside my door. I pulled it out and released the blade. There was enough light for me to see the doorknob. I focused on it, waiting for it to move. Instead, there was a loud knock.

"Paula. Are you in there?"

It was my stepdad.

"Yes." I retracted the blade and put the knife back under my pillow.

"Your mom called and said she's gonna be late. I made a salad and some pasta for dinner. Are you coming down?"

"Okay. In a minute."

"Dylan and I have already eaten. I'll leave a plate on the table for you. Try not to let it get cold."

"I won't. Thanks, Michael."

That little scare made me realize that I had no real idea how to use that knife to defend myself. I was pretty sure that I wasn't even holding the Vikov — that was its name — properly. If it was going to be of any use to me, then I'd have to learn how to use it.

I remembered that I'd seen a martial arts DVD in a box of videos Dylan brought with him. At the time, he told me to help myself to any of them I wanted to watch. When I was in the house alone, I went into his room and found it. It wasn't about knife fighting, but something called Eskrina, which is Filipino stick fighting. The tape wasn't even in English. There were quite a few ads in the video about the different kinds of training videos you could buy from this martial arts school. One of the ads showed a student dressed like a ninja with an instructor demonstrating how to grip a knife. He held it the way you hold a hammer, with the blade straight up and a really strong grip on the handle. The ad also showed maybe twenty students standing in front of large, human-sized foam blocks and practicing stabbing and slashing while instructors watched them and made suggestions. That was all they showed, but it was a start for me.

I couldn't find any foam blocks around the house, but we had a lot of cardboard boxes in the garage. I drew targets on a box with a marker pen, then stood like the ninjas in the video, one foot forward — the same one as the hand holding the knife, my left — and one foot back. I practiced stabbing and slashing at the boxes. Once I got the hang of staying balanced, I became really good, really fast. It was amazing how little noise the knife made when you used it properly. It sounded and felt like I was stabbing into a huge pile of jelly. I wondered if it would be the same stabbing a person. I didn't want to stab anyone, but I was prepared to do it if they were going to hurt me.

What Do You Think?

Kinsmen Arena

Later that week, Jobbi wore his school's hockey sweater for the first time. He didn't really know if the coaches wanted him to play or not until that afternoon when Mr. Dixon stopped him in the hallway to let him know that he was dressing for the game. Victor was happy for an excuse to get out of the house and go with his cousin to the game. They rode the city bus to the Kinsmen Arena. Vic carried Jobbi's stick.

The game didn't start too well. The other team scored a goal on each of Jobbi's first two shifts on the ice. Standing just behind the players' bench, Victor could hear Coach West demanding that Jobbi check harder. Victor also noticed that every time a player named Twerndon came back to the bench, he tapped his stick on Jobbi's kneepads to encourage him and to keep his spirits up.

Incredibly, the other team never scored another goal. With two minutes left in the game, the score was still 2 – 0. Eastside took a penalty just then, giving Central a power play. Coach West spoke into the ear hole of Jobbi's helmet. To the surprise of the players on the bench, the assistant coaches, and everyone watching, Jobbi hopped out of the gate and skate-danced, in his unusual style, out to the faceoff circle for the power play. Twerndon saw him coming out and seemed glad for the break, as he had been double-shifting for most of the period. As they passed one another, Twerndon tapped Jobbi's pads and quietly said to him, "Go to the net." As soon as the puck was dropped Jobbi skated straight toward the Eastside goal. Suddenly, he looked down and there at his feet, completely motionless, was the puck. Jobbi took it on his stick, made two hopping strides, spun and shot the puck into a wide-open side of the net. The whistle blew. Jobbi didn't seem to realize that he had scored. He was turning away from the goal when an Eastside defenceman crosschecked him hard from behind, sending him crashing to the ice. Victor thought he might be seriously hurt, but Jobbi got up quickly. A teammate wrestled with the Eastside player who'd crosschecked Jobbi. Both were given penalties.

Jobbi skated toward the bench, but before he got there, one of the assistant coaches pointed to the centre ice faceoff circle to indicate that Jobbi should stay on the ice. Jobbi looked to Coach West who nodded his approval.

From the faceoff at centre ice, the play moved immediately down to the Eastside goal. Both Jobbi and Shumzicky had good shots. The goalie juggled Jobbi's shot, which wasn't that hard but was in a difficult spot to catch. Later, Shumzicky gambled that he could beat his opponent to a loose puck. As a defenceman, he was the last man back. The Eastside player got to the puck first, tapping it past Shumzicky and starting up the ice. It appeared that no one would be able to catch him. Jobbi was the closest and had a small angle to his advantage, but the Eastside player was pulling away quickly. Jobbi took three strong strides, which looked more like windmill kicks. He then put all of his weight on his extended front leg while dragging the other leg behind him in a pose Vic was sure he'd seen in a figure skating competition. Then, reaching his stick out to its full length and holding it at the very end with only two fingers, Jobbi managed to flick the puck off the opponent's stick from well behind. Central took control and raced back up the ice, but the game ended before they could get another shot.

All the way home on the bus Victor couldn't stop shaking his head or ruffling his cousin's hair.

"I have never seen anyone play hockey like that before. I do not think anyone has. Not around here! But somehow, do not ask me how, you almost won the game — you, you *bunyock*!"

Victor noticed that it made his cousin happy to see him happy. He realized that he'd been pretty gloomy since he'd returned home from school.

A couple of nights later, when Jobbi arrived home after practice, Victor was in the basement with three friends, drinking beer and watching football.

Vic introduced Jobbi as his cousin, the hockey star. His friends looked at Jobbi and thought Victor was making fun of them. He guaranteed them he was not.

"It is true. He really gets the job done on the ice. He is a true Latvian like that."

They wanted Jobbi to join them for a beer, which Victor could see his cousin did not want to do. Just then, Vic's mom called down to say that Jobbi's mother was on the phone upstairs. Jobbi raced up. He hadn't heard from his mother or father in several weeks. Unfortunately things weren't good in Valmiera. Taska had been unable to find Michalenkov. Jobbi's father was to be tried and sentenced any day. Taska had heard that two years in prison was being considered. She had tried everything she could think of to help the situation, but had all but given up hope. They would have to pray that the judge would be lenient with his father. The horror of Taylus actually going to jail for something he didn't do was more than either of them could bear. Jobbi and his mother exchanged sorrow-filled goodbyes.

Despite his age, Jobbi understood how the politics of his country worked. Aija's father was the kind of man who made the laws in Latvia and Jobbi's father was the kind of man who had to follow them. There was very little anyone could do if Aija's father wanted someone to go to jail. And for hurting his daughter as she had been hurt, someone was going to pay. If they couldn't catch the real criminal, the next closest person they could catch would have to do. Taska had an old uncle, Romerus, who was an original member of the LNNK — the Latvian National Independence Movement. He used what influence he had to spare Taska from being involved in the proceedings, but he could do nothing for Taylus.

When Jobbi returned to the basement, Victor could tell he was troubled. Vic's friends, now drunk, tried again to get Jobbi to have a beer with them. Vic coaxed them all back to the television and let Jobbi escape to his room.

Jobbi's heart was so heavy when he went to bed that he had trouble getting to sleep. When he did sleep, his dreams were confused and unsettling . . . *until out of nowhere, a match, one for the other, revealed itself.*

The next morning, Jobbi delivered his papers in record time. When he was done, he rushed home and down to the basement to wake Victor. Vic had slept on the basement couch and woke up groggy and hung-over. Still, he could tell that there was something up with Jobbi who was speaking fast and mixing Latvian in with Russian and English. It was a little hard for Victor to understand in his half-awake, hung-over state. He asked Jobbi to stop for a second, then went to the bathroom, washed his face and asked him to start again — this time in English. That took longer, and when Jobbi was done, his idea sounded so far-fetched that Vic agreed to help him, obviously believing that it was never really going to happen anyway.

Two days later, however, Victor was at the International Airport boarding an Aeroflot Ilyushin ll-96 jet bound for Riga, Latvia.

Dumb Question Ask Another

Stephanie

One week before the dance, Mr. Wickens calls me to his office. He is way nervous and wants to know what progress I've made. I start telling him about the arrangements for the music and the decorating committee, but he stops me.

"That's all fine, but what about people? Is anyone going to show up? And what about some of those promises you made to me, Stephanie? How this dance might help to calm things down?"

Before I can answer, he just keeps going.

"We've been having some trouble in the school that you may or may not know about. It's the kind of trouble that could very well show up at your dance. I don't mind telling you, Stephanie, that if the police have to be called, at any time, there are going to be serious consequences." He pauses. "Very serious. Run along now, and do your best, Miss Horner. I know you're trying."

Pressure much! Yikes. I don't know what kind of trouble Mr. Wickens is talking about, but, ok, I did hear that the police were in the school this past weekend and that they'd checked every single locker. My first thought is that they're searching for drugs, but Jenny Harris, whose dad is a policeman, shakes her head when I say that at our lunch table. She whispers in my direction, "Weapons."

I gave Kevin the job of making sure that any social outsider, or anyone who felt like an outsider, came to the dance. Kevin has really changed. He seems proud to be considered a geek or a nerd these days. Being Jobbi's best friend has given him a lot of confidence. I know that he's talked to all the socially challenged kids in junior high, girl or boy, and invited them to the dance. He does it by convincing them that the dance will be fun for everyone. I even spot him giving some seriously uncoordinated grade-seven boys a dance lesson in the hallway. Kevin is stomping around and the three of them are trying to copy him. None of them looks very good, including Kevin. I'm not sure what Kevin knows about dancing — although that's probably not such a big deal. Dances have been cancelled for so long that none of us have ever been to one.

I notice the new girl, Soon Lee, standing beside me. We smile at one another. I ask her if she will be coming. "I have already tickets to go and hear Celine Dion sing that evening." She doesn't smile or frown, but looks at me as though she wants me to say something about her situation. "That's too bad you can't come, Soon. It's definitely going to be fun."

Because Kevin is doing such a good job at inviting the so'challs, a lot of the other kids are becoming concerned that the dance will be some kind of nerd fest. I'm having so many problems at this point that I find Jesse and talk to him about it. He comes up with the really cool idea of having a dancing contest.

My friend, Melinda, says that she'll get a trophy from her father's sporting goods store for the prize. The idea definitely gets some interest, especially from the girls who are good dancers, but what catches the attention of the whole school is the news that two young, single teachers — Mr. Natterly, history and Ms. Applebaum, art — are thinking of joining in on the contest! The only problem is that they haven't actually said so. So far, they've only agreed to be part of the supervisory staff. It's another one of Jobbi's strange *Twilight Zone* moments that gets them involved.

As soon as I mention the dance contest, Jobbi suddenly notices something really interesting high up on the far wall. He even twists his head around as though he's trying to see whatever it is he sees, upside down. I look too, but I don't see a thing. Anyway, after he stares at the wall for a minute or so with his mouth open, he blurts out, "Natarrrlie 'nd Uppullboom," with one of those big-eared, goofy smiles on his face. To make a long story short, before I can talk to either teacher about it, the rumour races through the school and no one is more surprised by it than the teachers themselves.

Then after lunch the next day, while the hallways are full of kids getting ready for afternoon classes, Mr. Natterly spots Ms. Applebaum walking toward him. She's carrying this big armload of papers. Right out of the blue, Mr. Natterly, who's tall, reaches out for Ms. Applebaum's free hand and lifts it high into the air. Ms. Applebaum is kinda freaked for maybe a second, but she catches on fast. She ends up doing — not one, but like, two — delicate twirls under his arm.

When Ms. Applebaum is done, Mr. Natterly lets go of her hand and does this super cool, low bow to her, and she curtsies in return. Then they smile at one another and head out on their separate their ways. Wow! After that, every kid in the school wants to be at the dance just to see those two together in the dance contest. I have a feeling it's going to be a sell-out.

Even though I'm close to fulfilling my promise to Mr. Wickens to have everyone in the school attend the dance, I have this real anxious, nagging feeling in my stomach. Jobbi has no idea how much I'm counting on him to make this dance work and to bring the school together. There is no doubt in my mind that he can do it. What worries me is whether he will actually be there when I need him.

In Your Dreams

Soon Lee

Hailey is my online friend. Her username on the Internet is Hailey_m51p, which is unique and easy to recognize. I am recognized as Iseul88. She and I have been friends since I lived in Singapore although we have never seen one another. We enjoy listening to the same pop singers. Hailey_m51p is in the Celine Dion Site forum when I post that I would be attending the Celine concert here where I live. Everyone on the forum is excited to hear the news and asking that I will tell them everything that happens and all of the songs she sings. I too am quite excited. After the topic changes, Hailey sends me a private message.

<what's up?>

She may have noticed a small reluctance in the replies I made to other forum members who were congratulating me. I tell Hailey of the dance.

<you can't miss CD for a dance!// UNLESS . . . >

Hailey is two years older than I and lives in Gainesville, Florida.

< . . . there is a certain boy??>

I send her a goofy smile 8-) because she is correct — there *is*. She knows I have some difficulty to find friends.

<tell me all about him>

I tell her of a funny, clumsy boy I have noticed. How he causes me to smile inwardly when I see him walking in front of me — swaying to and fro like a metronome. That I overhear other girls say they find him to be *cool.* I wanted only to say a little bit but I cannot stop talking on my keyboard.

<wow! he sounds perfect for you>

Hailey has told me before that she would enjoy having a boyfriend. She has also told me that it is hard for her, but not why it is so. I do not ask as I know there are some things about her which she does not wish to share, although I am very curious.

<does he have a girlfriend?>

I tell her I'm not certain because this boy is often in the presence of a popular girl.

<that means nothing! you must go the to dance>

I am very surprised to hear this because Hailey is a most devoted follower of Celine Dion. She would give everything to attend such a concert. Hailey has never travelled very far from Gainesville and does not believe Celine Dion will ever come there. I tell her that my mother has spent a great deal of money for our tickets. She won't take my father because he will only fall asleep and begin snoring.

<lmfao ;-} but if you don't go to the dance how will the boy ever notice you??>

Regrettably, it is true that he has not seen me in the way that I would like. He is very busy and popular.

<you will have many chances to see CD//are you happy to let him find another girlfriend?>

I respond to my friend that even if I did go to the dance, how or why would he notice me?

<you must ask him to dance>

This I cannot do as I would not feel right to be so forward.

<then you must do what I do//bump him with your footrest>

<foot>

How strange. I decide I must search for a meaning of m51p.

<go to the dance Iseul88//please>

<for <3 *me?* >

Well, Maybe

Valmiera, Latvia

Victor took a bus from the Riga International Airport all the way to Valmiera. The ride took more than four hours, with what seemed like a hundred stops along the way. He had an address for his aunt, but that was all. As far as he knew, she didn't know that he was coming. He had left a note for his parents stating only that he would be gone for a few days, but didn't say where. He intended to call them once he'd accomplished his task. Jobbi asked him to do one thing there. He wanted Victor to rent a car and drive his mother to the Jumikis farm, where Aija and Boris had been wed more than a year earlier. Jobbi wanted his mother to speak to Aija Jumikis and explain to her what had happened to his father.

Taska couldn't believe her eyes when she saw Victor at her door. She gave him a huge hug. As for Victor, he patted her on the back and repeated the only comforting Latvian words he could think of, "There, there, Auntie Taska. There, there."

The next day, Victor went with his aunt to visit Taylus in jail. It turned out to be more of a shelter than an actual jail. The security let Taylus out so he could go for an espresso with his visitors. Victor never thought of himself as an emotional guy, but he found it hard not to tear up, watching his aunt and his uncle say goodbye after holding on to one another through the whole visit.

Although Victor had only been in Latvia for a little over a day he was surprised to discover how much of the language he could understand when it was spoken to him. He was even more surprised to find that he was capable of responding in short phrases. He guessed that something must have sunk in while listening to his parents for all those years.

On Victor's third day there, he rented a Renault Clio and drove his aunt to the Jumikis villa. She didn't really want to go until he explained to her that it was Jobbi's wish, and that Jobbi had sent him all this way to help her do it. Taska knew her son well enough to understand how important this must be to him. During the drive to the villa, she recounted the details of her unsuccessful attempt at matchmaking.

When they got to the Jumikis estate, Taska knocked on the door of the main house twice. After the second knock, the door flew open and a large, elderly woman appeared. Victor couldn't hear what was being said, but he could tell that the large woman was trying to get out of the doorway, but she couldn't because something, or someone, inside the house was restraining her. Taska was clearly taken aback by the woman's anger. She had been Mrs. Jumikis' aesthetician and friend for many years. After all, they had conspired together to find Aija a husband.

When Victor got out of the car to go to his aunt's aid, he caught sight of a girl leaving the property on a mountain bike heading toward the town. She wore a shiny silver cycling helmet, a light blue vest and long red sleeves.

Meanwhile, the angry woman in the doorway suddenly closed her eyes and collapsed. Taska rushed to her side, as did people from inside the house. Victor suspected that the woman who collapsed was Aija's grandmother, and it had been Aija's mother who was trying to restrain the agitated elderly woman.

Victor helped to carry the grandmother into the sitting room. A housekeeper in uniform and a handyman carrying a hammer appeared, as did another woman in uniform. All of them were concerned about the grandmother and alternately glaring at Victor and Taska.

Soon, the older woman began to come around. Someone else rushed into the room with a cup of tea. Victor took his aunt's elbow and tried to steer her slowly back toward the door. The younger woman, who was certainly Aija's mother, turned on both of them.

"We trusted you! All of us — my mother, my daughter, my husband and me. Shame on you. Leave this house!"

Taska didn't want to leave without saying what she had planned to say, but it was obvious that no one was interested in listening to her under those conditions. They left quietly.

On the way back to Valka, Vic wondered what Jobbi had been thinking. But when he thought about it again, Jobbi had asked him to take his mother to see Aija Jumikis — not her family. That was probably Aija he'd seen leaving on the bicycle.

From the moment Victor had stepped onto the airplane at the airport, he had a strong feeling that he might have an important purpose in this whole affair. But what that purpose was, he had no idea. There was still a half day of rental time on the car, so after dropping Taska at her apartment, Victor returned to Valmiera to see if he could find Aija Jumikis and her bicycle. Maybe there was something he could do to help his cousin and his family by speaking with her himself.

Not A Chance

Kevin

Me and Stephanie are eating lunch together on the Friday before the dance. All around us we hear kids making plans for next Thursday. The excitement is definitely building. Every kid in the school is planning to be there. Jobbi told me that even the hockey players are talking about coming back to the school right after their game, which ends around 7:00. It's the first league game of the season.

Not all the news is good, though. There are rumours all over the place about kids planning to settle scores with other kids during the dance. Stephanie says she hears that the Dixie Road girls are after somebody and planning to get whoever it is during the dance. I overheard two grade-nine guys threatening each other in the hallway toilets. It was over a girl, and their last words were that they'd see each other at the dance.

It's too bad stuff like that is still happening, because ever since the dance was announced, life at school has improved quite a bit. Most kids are really looking forward to it. I find it strange that Steph, who tends to worry about things like the colour of her pens matching her ring binder, isn't all that concerned about the possibility of trouble. I guess that's because she has some kind of a plan. She finally tells me what it is while we're eating.

"Remember when I asked Jobbi and you to help me at the door during the dance?"

I nod, 'cause I'm munching on my cheese, lettuce and mayo sandwich.

"Well, it wasn't really selling tickets that I wanted help with." She pauses and looks straight at me. "I want Jobbi to pick a dance partner for, like, every person that comes to the dance."

Steph has this big smile on her face, but I can see she isn't joking. She is completely serious. I don't get it. "Why would you want Jobbi to pick who dances with who, Steph?"

"Because he's really good at it."

"Wow. I don't know. That doesn't sound like that good of an idea to me. Not unless you want to see Jobbi get slapped silly by Pinger or Rena, or maybe both of them working him over tag team." Which is a much more possible outcome.

"But that's just it. He won't get beat up because he's good at picking girls and guys who get along well together. Really, really good. Remember volleyball — when Jobbi picked those fun teams? And Natterly and Applebaum? That was Jobbi too. And I've seen him do so much other stuff!"

I had to admit that Jobbi does have this weird sort of awareness — or something — about the girls I mention to him. "Maybe. But I'm not even sure that Jobbi knows that he can do that sort of stuff. Whatever *that* is."

"You're right about that, Kevin; Jobbi definitely does not realize he can do it. He doesn't know there's anything special about him. But I do. And it's very, very important that we don't tell him."

"If we don't tell him, then what's the point?"

"If I told Jobbi what I thought he could do, he would so not believe it. And he probably wouldn't want to help then, because he wouldn't, like, I don't know . . . trust himself . . . or something."

"Okay, so we don't tell him. But even if you do somehow convince him to pick dance partners for everyone, nobody in this school is going to go along with what he says. They'll all think it's a joke, or that you're making fun of them."

"Hmm. That's true . . . "

"Kids would probably trust a Ouija Board more than they'd trust Jobbi."

"A *wee-what*? What was that Kevin?

"Well, only that, kids would rather trust a Ouija Board than Jobbi . . . Hey, did you know they're real, and that most people don't know how to use one properly? They always . . . "

"That game where you put your fingers on the little table and you ask it a question?"

"Yeah, that's it. I use mine all the time."

"For what? What do you consult a Ouija Board about?"

"Oh. Uh. Um . . . *stuff* . . . *sigh*. Girls. Mostly."

"Girls? How odd. That won't work. It would take too long for every kid to go through. We need something that works faster."

"Hey, in case you haven't noticed Steph, this whole idea of yours is odd."

I seem to catch Steph by surprise saying that. She just stares at me for a while. Then she says, "That's true. It is a bit odd, isn't it? Maybe we shouldn't try to pretend that it's not."

"What do you mean?"

"The idea of this dance is a bit odd, I know, but it's also about taking a chance and having some fun doing it. Maybe we should just call it what it is, An Odd Dance . . . or Slightly Odd Event?"

" Or, we could call it *The Odd Ball*." I smile at her. "Get it?"

"Yeah, hey, not bad, Kevin."

"And speaking of odd, my brother has one of those answer balls that you ask a yes or no question, then when you turn it around, an answer is written inside this little window?"

"An Eight Ball, right? Kevin, that sounds perfect."

"Um, I don't think that's what it's called. But I'm pretty sure it works on the same principle."

"Would your brother let us use it for the dance?"

"He doesn't really let me touch his stuff, but . . . he has been bugging me to let him use my nitro truck. I think I can make a trade with him."

"You have a nitro-fuelled truck?"

"RC — that means remote control. Don't worry. I'll get the answer ball one way or another." I slap my fist into the palm of my other hand. Steph rolls her eyes. We both laugh.

"We'll have to show Jobbi how to use it to pick dance partners."

"Sure. No problem, Steph."

Steph is pretty sure the answer ball idea is going to work. I'm not quite as sure — at least to begin with — but the more I think about it, the more obvious it is that if anyone can use an answer ball properly, it would probably be Jobbi.

"Now we need to find a way to get the partners to see each other the way Jobbi sees them. What about a special dance — a special partners dance!"

"Mmm. A *special partners dance* sounds a little lame, don't you think? If you're going to go with the Odd Ball, then why not go all the way? Get the DJ to call it an *oddball dance*. That way everyone will know that it's not anything all that serious."

"Would *you* take part in something called an *oddball dance*, Kevin?"

"Of course. I'd love to."

"So would I."

It was like we'd solved a huge problem — and it felt good. "But what happens if someone doesn't want to dance with the person Jobbi picks? Then what? You know that's for sure going to happen, Steph. I mean, depending on how many kids don't want to go along, this whole idea could really backfire, couldn't it?"

"Yeah. Things could definitely backfire. But I also totally believe that we all have someone we fit well with. The problem is that we don't always, like, *know* how to find that person. We're too shy or too afraid or too busy or too confused to realize that someone — maybe even right in our own class — could be perfect for us. Sometimes it takes someone else to open our eyes. That's exactly what Jobbi can do. I've seen him do it. And I'm sure he can do it again. I believe in him."

She looks at me, searching for my reaction. I'm remembering all the times I'd asked Jobbi about certain girls and he'd always say, "Not for me so much." It never occurred to me to ask him who he thought would be "for me so much." I sure hadn't figured him out the way Steph had. But I'm still not as completely convinced as she is that everything will work out the way she hopes.

"It's just one dance, Kevin . . . *one little dance*. No one is, like, getting married for life or anything. It's supposed to be fun and it's up to us to make sure that everyone sees it that way. I think calling the dance The Odd Ball will help. Jobbi and the answer ball will totally do the rest. Trust me."

Steph looked at the clock on the wall of the lunchroom.

"The Odd Ball. Holy buttons, I have to make some new posters. And, Kevin, remember: all anyone will know is that the answer ball is doing all the picking of dance partners.

"Even Jobbi?"

"Especially Jobbi. We don't say anything to him about our plan. When he arrives to help us at the door, we just show him how the ball works."

"But I don't even know how to use it for something like this. A hundred-and-eighty — or more — kids! I don't think the answer ball was designed for something like that. It might, I don't know, overheat or blow up or completely shut down!"

"Trust me, Kevin. Jobbi will know how to handle it. It'll be fun for him."

"But what if Jobbi freezes up when a girl comes to the table and he can't think of any names. That happens to some guys, you know. They freeze up around girls."

Steph smiles and does that head-tilting thing.

"That won't happen to Jobbi, Kevin. Believe me. Besides, he'll have the student list to use. It'll be fine. Jobbi will do it all." She looks right at me. "I know you're worried Kevin. So am I. But everyone just *has* to go along with this. If they don't, this whole school could come apart."

Obviously

1142 Hillcrest Ave.

Jobbi did not know precisely when he would be going to jail. He was sure, however, that he would end up there very soon. The reason was that he had used the money he had collected from his newspaper customers to buy the airplane ticket to Riga. Victor was not aware of it at the time. He was curious, but decided not to ask questions. If he had known from where the money had come, he probably wouldn't have gone. Jobbi also gave Victor what other money he had, including a year's worth of saved tips given to him by his customers. Altogether, he spent or gave Victor about eleven-hundred dollars. Jobbi now owed the newspaper $638.50 and was expected to deliver that amount to his district manager at eight o'clock Friday evening.

Jobbi showed up at the usual street corner looking like a man on his way to the gallows. He confessed to his manager that he didn't have the money he was supposed to have, none of it, not a cent. When the manager asked where it was, Jobbi only shrugged. There were several more questions after that one, each more accusatory, all of which Jobbi met with no response. The older man finally gave up asking questions.

After a heavy sigh, he told Jobbi that he was in big trouble, but that he also needed him to keep delivering his papers, every morning, until he could find someone else to take over his delivery route. Jobbi nodded, indicating that he would do that, and walked away not sure of how he should feel, since it seemed that he wasn't going to jail immediately. He also guessed that this was not the first time his manager had had to deal with a paper carrier who did not have the money from his customer bill collection.

When Jobbi returned home from his paper deliveries the next morning, his aunt was waiting for him at the door. She asked him to come into the living room. Sitting on the couch was his uncle, who usually worked Saturday mornings, but had stayed home today. Also in the room with him was the district circulation manager for the Sun newspaper. The newspaperman was standing and putting something into his inside jacket pocket when Jobbi entered. He spoke first. "Jobbi. It looks like your aunt and uncle here want you to keep your job. I want you to also, but let me warn you, don't ever be out on your bill again — not even a cent — or I will not hesitate to bring in the police." He looked Jobbi in the eye. "Do you understand me, son?"

Jobbi nodded. "Ahyess. Hi underrrstoods."

When the manager had gone, Jobbi's uncle pointed to an armchair and Jobbi sat in it. Jobbi could see that his uncle was trying to keep his composure, but as he spoke about what Jobbi had done, he became more and more angry.

It turned out that his aunt and uncle had been saving the paper route earnings that Jobbi had been giving them every two weeks. The money was supposed to be for his room and board, but they knew he would need it sometime and had kept it for him. They used that money to pay the district manager what Jobbi owed. His uncle scolded him, saying that the money could have been used for many other things, including helping his mother and father in Latvia.

In addition, his uncle told Jobbi that he was disappointed in him. He was disappointed that Jobbi had lost the trust of the people he worked for and also the trust of the people who cared about him. After that he asked Jobbi what he had done with the money but Jobbi remained silent, fearing they would insist that Victor return to Canada before he could accomplish what he went there to do. His uncle shook his head and explained that as with all misbehaviour, there would be consequences — no more hockey or going out after school until they felt that he clearly understood the seriousness of what he had done.

His uncle turned his back, which was the signal for Jobbi to remove himself from the room. Jobbi apologized in Latvian, which was acknowledged by a shrug of his uncle's shoulders while keeping his back to his nephew.. This became an opportunity for his aunt to quietly give Jobbi a hug and let him know that he was still loved.

Jobbi made his way down to his room with what felt like all the cares of the world on his shoulders. The penalty was severe, though not as severe as going to jail. The consequences of the punishment were serious, too. Jobbi could barely face the thought of telling his teammates and his friends, Kevin and Stephanie, that he would not be with them on Thursday night. More trust lost, he realized. Trust that he might never have a chance to regain.

Jobbi had endured, and continued to endure, a prolonged separation from his home and his parents. He had suffered the kind of emotional stress that a young person should never have to absorb. He had lived daily with communication problems and fought persistent physical and emotional bullying. He had survived desperate loneliness. Yet, the next week of school would be the most difficult time of his life by far.

Oh, Please

Kevin

When I meet Jobbi on the corner Monday morning, he definitely isn't his usual self. I expected him to feel good about being on the hockey team and having the respect of not just the geeks, but all the kids — and also about not being bullied by Wally or Pinger anymore. Instead, he looks as though he doesn't have much to live for. I have no idea what is going on, but I try to cheer him up anyway. Nothing works. I'm guessing that it's not the best time to ask him about a girlfriend for me.

Stephanie finds us at our lockers. She's excited about getting three more entries for the dance contest. That's when Jobbi tells us about his aunt and uncle's decision.

"Hiam sauhrrry, Stayfoonie, boat hi cane note be vit chyou on dis donce nyight."

"What? You can't be at the dance?" I ask him.

"Noah, hiam note pairrrmit tew goa owt by mwhy honkel und haunty."

I blow up.

"Your uncle and aunt can't do that to you! They have no right! Do they have any idea what they're doing? To all of us?

To this school? I'm going to come to your house and talk to them, Jobbi. I'll be nice and I'll explain how tough it's been for you and how, when you're just starting to fit into . . . "

Without lifting his eyes Jobbi shakes his head, overriding my plan and putting the brakes on my anger.

"Chyou muz note do dis, Kaveen. Dey arrres in darrrer rrrites tew do dis. Hit's mwy behaveeorrr dat haas coazed dem tew saya soa."

He doesn't tell us about the newspaper money or the airplane ticket he'd spent it on. I don't find out about that stuff until long after.

Jobbi keeps his eyes on the ground the whole time. When he finally lifts his head, I'm pacing around in a circle with my hands on my hips. I can hardly contain myself. Stephanie, though, stands there perfectly still, hugging some books to her with both arms. She's staring at Jobbi with this intense expression of disbelief. She starts shaking her head and I can see that she's trying to say something, but obviously can't find the words. I get this crazy feeling that she isn't completely surprised by what Jobbi just told us, yet at the same time, she can't believe that it's actually happening. Judging by how upset Steph is, it must have been really hard for Jobbi to tell her.

Finally, Steph seems to accept that Jobbi won't be there to help her on the night of the dance. She turns and runs down the hall without saying a word to him. Jobbi knows that she's disappointed and that she's probably feeling betrayed. He spins around and smashes a fist into his locker door. I say the most obvious thing that comes to my mind.

"Wow, man. I think you've lost your chance with her."

Who Cares

Stephanie

I've heard and read about people who feel as though the whole world is crumbling around them — usually because of something terrible happening. My situation isn't that bad, but I definitely feel like my world is crumbling around me. I start to think of ways that I can cancel the dance. I don't want to be responsible for what could happen now that my plan has been totally destroyed by one person. Without Jobbi there, anything can happen — fights, vandalism, police, Mr. Wickens getting in trouble and a million of the other things that are already happening in this place every day. The dance is going to be a complete disaster and end up accomplishing the exact opposite of what I was trying to do.

But that isn't the only thing that makes me feel like giving up. I've been hoping for a while that Jobbi might like me. I mean, it isn't hard to see that he gets a little weird when I'm around. I guess I mean weir-*der*, than he normally is. But that's the thing about him. He only *seems* weird because of his accent and coming from another country. Once I started to figure him out, I saw that he was totally one of the nicest, gentlest guys in the whole school. And then, when I looked even closer, I discovered that he has brains and courage and character too. I admire him for that, and I was hoping that with his help we might be able to change things around here. And I thought he and I were becoming, you know, more than just friends.

That feeling is totally gone now. Maybe he really is just your average, only-concerned-with-himself type of guy. I mean, if he really did care about me, he wouldn't let me down when I need him. I might not be the brightest bulb on the Christmas tree, but I'd never let down someone I care about. Never.

When Jobbi tells me he won't be at the door for the dance, I just turn and run away from him as far as I can get. I end up at the back-corner study cubicle in the school library. I throw my books down, collapse into the chair, put my head on my arms and cry. It's not the first time I've been here, nor am I the only girl in the school to use this place to hide, or leave tear stains on the desktop.

I'm so upset and confused that I don't even know how long I've been here. It feels like I could have missed a class, or even two. When I lift my head and check over my shoulder, I can't believe who is on the other side of the book stack, the last person I want to see right then — Ms. Dufault. She only has to take one look to know she was right not to put her trust in me. At this moment I also have no idea what I'm going to do about the dance that is only three days away. She did say to let her know when I wanted to cancel. Maybe it's time to pull the plug on everything. I dry my face on my sleeve and go to talk to her, totally prepared to accept her gloating.

Ms. Dufault can tell right away that I've been crying.

"Stephanie! What's wrong? Is it that boy I've seen you with who caused these tears?"

I can't even answer without more tears coming, so I shake my head.

"Oh. Well, I imagine you're overwhelmed by everything you've taken on." She sighs. "Let me guess. Right now, you're probably at the point where you're discovering that you don't have enough time to get everything done that needs doing."

I nod.

"And suddenly, just when you need them most, everyone you were really counting on has disappeared?"

That's so true I almost burst into tears — again.

She finds a tissue in her book bag and hands it to me.

"That's not any great insight on my part, Stephanie. We've all been there many times. By we, I mean we women who take our responsibilities seriously. What you're actually learning here is that, in the end, the only person you can really count on is yourself."

I don't know how to bring up the subject of cancelling the dance without blubbering like a little kid. Ms. Dufault looks at me a little more intently.

"But you're not overwhelmed, are you, Stephanie? Not really. Uh-uh. I don't think that's it at all." She sighs again, heavily this time. "It is the boy that's got you in this state, isn't it?"

I shake my head to deny it, out of embarrassment I suppose, but she isn't fooled.

"It's not enough that they disappoint you, but they have to rip out your heart while they're about it, don't they?"

She puts her hand on the side of my head and smoothes out some of my hair while looking into my face. "You should finish crying and get back to class." She doesn't say, "Young girls can be so foolish," but I can see it in her eyes. She does say, "It's not too late to cancel, you know. I can speak to Principal Largent for you, if you'd like me to?"

I still have no idea what I'm going to do about the dance, but I suddenly decide not to accept her offer. Despite what happened with Jobbi today, I'm beginning to realize that deep inside me, I don't want to believe what Ms. Dufault believes — about Jobbi, or about me. I shake my head. She shrugs her shoulders and makes one last comment that does surprise me.

"Well, good luck then, Stephanie. I will be there Thursday. That, you *can* count on."

Yeah, Right

Paula

Every day, it gets harder and harder to know who I can trust. Everywhere I look, I think I see kids either watching me or talking about me. Some of them are definitely looking for a chance to mess me up. I try to make sure that I don't get cornered alone in a bathroom or an empty classroom.

The teachers make a point of ignoring me because they don't like the way I dress. Earlier today, I saw Vice-Principal Wickens talking to that stressed-out Stephanie chick. They both shut up and watched me when I passed, and didn't start talking again until I couldn't hear what they were saying. When I think about it, I remember seeing Stephanie getting cozy with the freakin' Dixie Roaders in the lunchroom. I don't know what her problem is with me. Maybe she's jealous like all the other girls. Who knows? But she doesn't look that tough. I'm pretty sure I could handle her even without the Vikov. Hey — maybe that's why Miss Stressball was talking with the gang; she was recruiting them to do her dirty work for her.

I could really use a boyfriend — a big, strong guy I could trust. He could carry the knife and protect both of us with it.

Maybe even scare my stepbrother. But for all the guys who like to talk and hang around, you'd think at least one of them would've asked me to be his girlfriend, or at least to go out on a date?

It's definitely not my fault. I mean, I didn't chase anyone away intentionally. I'd go out with just about anyone who asked me — except maybe that Kevin guy. He's way too confident for a geek. Crap, I might even go out with him if there was no one else.

Maybe I come across as too hot for most of those guys, like I'm way out of their league or something? I don't mean to do that. I'd probably be better off with one of the older guys from senior high, someone who doesn't get intimidated so easily.

The teachers and principals are still all over the school looking for the knife. They've done one total locker search and it looks like they're getting ready to do another one. I've seen Mr. Drew and Mr. Wickens doing random backpack checks on some of the guys. They still don't suspect it might be a girl. That's good, because I'm pretty sure it won't be long before I'll have to use the knife to protect myself. I'm ready for that. I have to be.

You Wish

1142 Hillcrest Ave.

During that final week of school before Christmas break, Jobbi felt as though he was stuck inside a very unpleasant dream. Even spending time with Kevin was not the distraction it usually was for him. He got to see Stephanie in the hallways at school and in class. He badly wanted to make up with her, but he could see that she was determined to move on and leave him out of her plans. It was even harder for Jobbi when she did eventually acknowledge him, but not in the usual smiling way that he had come to look forward to every day. They did not talk or eat lunch together. He was completely removed from her life.

As for hockey, Jobbi was surprised at what little impression his withdrawal from the team made on his coach. The players noticed, however. Jesse and Kris Cerps found him at his locker the next day and asked what was going on. He told them that his aunt and uncle wanted him to make some changes before he could return to hockey. Jesse told him not to worry about it because it happens to all players at one time or another, especially if you brought home some poor marks. He also told Jobbi that the trick was to get down to work on whatever they needed from him so he could return to practice as soon as possible.

"We need that scoring touch of yours, buddy."

Although it had taken him a while, Jobbi understood what Jesse meant by *scoring touch.* And, he desperately did want to return to practice and be part of the team, but he also knew that it was going to take a serious amount of time for his uncle and aunt to finally relent. Jobbi had no illusions about that and was resigned to being separated from everything in his new life that he cared about. He had even deeper concern for his cousin. If anything should happen to him on his journey, the consequences would be more than he or any of his family could bear. But Victurus also needed the time to find Aija. Jobbi hoped that, with Victor, she might help to find a solution to his parents' predicament.

Although he didn't have the spirit for it, Jobbi forced himself to study extra hard in that final week before Christmas. He was determined to win back the respect of his Canadian family as soon as possible. He followed all of their wishes carefully and kept his room and the whole basement neat. He shovelled the snow from the sidewalk and the driveway and insisted on washing and drying the supper dishes.

Despite his positive attempts at reconciliation, Jobbi's heart remained so heavy that it took a long time for him to fall asleep at night. Most nights it seemed as though he had only just closed his eyes when the clock alarm would ring to get him up to deliver his papers and go to school.

On the last Thursday before Christmas break, and the day of his hockey team's first game of the season — and the night of the dance that Stephanie had organized — Jobbi was so tired when he arrived home from school, he flopped onto his bed and immediately fell asleep. It wasn't long before he was awoken by his aunt shaking his shoulder. She was dressed in the clothes she wore to work. She didn't normally wake him this way, so Jobbi immediately sat up, fearing there was more bad news from Latvia. But what he heard was, "Jobbus. Victurus did not come home again today. I am very concerned. Do you know where our Victurus has gone?"

When Victors parents had first seen the simple note left by their son, they secretly hoped that he had decided to return to his school.

Jobbi and Victor had agreed that the less his parents knew of their plan the more chance they would have of succeeding. It would also save Victor's parents from unnecessary worry. But now his cousin had been gone for several days and Jobbi was also concerned about not hearing any news. There was no way that he was going to take the chance of not telling his aunt the truth now regardless of what the consequences might be. He was barely awake when he mumbled his reply in Latvian.

"He is in Latvia, Auntie."

"La . . . Latvia!" His aunt stammered in surprise. "Our Victurus! In Latvia?"

Jobbi explained that he had used the money from the newspapers to buy Victor an airplane ticket. His aunt appeared to be confused. The news of her son's whereabouts seemed completely impossible to her. She left Jobbi's room and rushed upstairs. She moved so fast that Jobbi thought she must have left something burning on the stove. Moments later, she returned to the basement with his uncle. He too stammered in Latvian, "Jobbus. Is, is this true? Victurus — our Victurus, is right now in . . . in Latvia?"

Jobbi confirmed that it was so and his aunt and uncle stared at one another, apparently quite unable to fully comprehend the meaning of this news. When he told them that he had asked Victor to go to Latvia, to help his mother and father, they looked at one another again, almost in shock.

"To help Taska and Taylus . . . ?" His uncle wasn't able to finish his thought because tears were coming to his eyes. He embraced his wife. After a few moments, they separated and both of them embraced Jobbi at the same time, words bubbling out of them . . .

"Victurus is gone home?"

"Victurus, our baby."

"Victurus with Taylus."

"Victurus with Taska."

"It . . . it is good. It is good. Yes. He will help them, Jobbi. He will help them!"

"Victurus is so smart. He will find a way. He will find a way to bring them to us."

They hugged Jobbi again and again. Jobbi began to understand that not only did this news not upset his relatives, it was a dream-come-true for them. As they slowly began to accept the reality of this unlikely turn of events, his uncle couldn't help shaking Jobbi's hand over and over. He was incredibly grateful to Jobbi, but Jobbi wasn't totally sure why. His uncle was so grateful, he spoke in English.

"Jobbi, you must play your hockey. When is it you must play again? We will come. Your aunt and me. We will come to see. To see you play the hockey."

"It is today, Uncle. At five-thirty," Jobbi answered in Latvian.

"It is ten minutes before five o'clock. It is still possible for you to play?"

"It is possible if you drive me, Uncle."

"I will. I most certainly will. Collect what you need and I will get my coat."

"And the dance afterwards, Uncle? May I go to the dance at my school after hockey also?"

"Dance? Dance, Jobbus! Of course. You must. You must certainly dance. Dance and be happy, Jobbus!"

When they got to the Southland rink, there were only ten minutes until game time. Jobbi met Coach West in the corridor. He told Jobbi that the official score sheet had already been handed in and because his name was not on it, he wouldn't be able to play. Jobbi's face fell in disappointment. Coach Dixon, however, had overheard what was being said from inside the dressing room. He came to the rescue.

"Coach West, I think I can fix that. When I handed in the game sheet, I told the scorekeeper about Craddock possibly showing up at the last minute from his dental appointment. He told me there was no problem as long as I got the name to him before the puck was dropped. I'll go and put Jobbi's name on the sheet right now. We'll certainly need him if Craddock doesn't make it." He rushed away, ignoring Coach West's mutterings about "player discipline" and "showing up whenever they damn well felt like it."

When he got into the dressing room, Jobbi received a hearty welcome from most of his teammates. He was happy about reconciling with his aunt and uncle and about not going to jail and about being able to play hockey, and he was also excited about being able to attend the dance with his good friends after the game. Jobbi's happiness showed in his skating. He floated and bobbed around the rink with more exuberance than he had ever shown before. He even caught the attention of the opposing team, Oak Park Secondary. None of their players had ever seen a skating style quite like Jobbi's. The Oak Park players gathered at centre ice during the warm-up just to watch him. Today it didn't bother Jobbi in the least to be the centre of attention. Instead, he decided that it felt good.

On his first shift of the game, Jobbi scored. Jumping high into the air to avoid a sandwiching attempt by the two Oak Park defencemen, Jobbi managed to accurately slide the puck between the goalie's skates. His Central teammates came off the bench and surrounded him in an ecstatic celebration. The team was immediately issued a bench penalty by the referee for delaying the game. Oak Park managed to score on the power play opportunity. 1 – 1

With only seconds left in the first period, an Oak Park defenceman attempted to shoot the puck down the ice to relieve the pressure the Central team was putting on their goal. Instead of going all the way down the ice, the puck hit Jobbi in the back. He winced, then quickly collected the puck onto his stick and made a rink-wide pass to a wide-open Jesse skating fast down the opposite boards. Jesse took the pass, faked a slap shot, and made a long return pass to Jobbi who was skating toward the net. The goalie had come well out of his net to try to meet Jesse's shot. He had no chance to recover before Jobbi redirected the perfectly executed return pass into the unguarded side of the goal. The end-of-period buzzer sounded a half-second after the puck crossed the goal line. 2 – 1, Central Secondary. End of the first period.

Despite his team playing well, Coach West was clearly not in a good mood. His plan to teach Principal Largent what a bad decision it was to institute academic requirements for hockey players, was backfiring. As head coach he'd replaced the star players who had withdrawn from the team because of it, with the worst player he'd seen at the tryouts. But now, instead of making the team into the embarrassment he thought they'd be, this skating kangaroo, Jobbi, had them holding their own!

Well, he could fix that. He kept Jobbi on the bench for the whole second period, which ended 3 – 2 for Oak Park after they scored twice within a minute.

In the third period, Central played furiously, hemming Oak Park in their own end for most of the period, but they were still unable to get the puck into the net. Then, with less than three minutes left, the two assistant coaches approached the head coach. After that short huddle, Jobbi was sent onto the ice for the first time since the opening period. He stayed on for the next two minutes and thirty seconds and was exhausted from skating hard on offence and then skating back even harder to play defence in front of his goalie. When he came to the bench for a change, Coach West casually waved him away and back into the game. Kris delayed the faceoff as long as he could so Jobbi could catch his breath.

The faceoff was in the Central zone. The puck was won by the Oak Park centre and sent back to his defenceman. Before the defenceman could get it, the edge of his skate got caught in an ice rut and he fell. Jobbi, who was closest, jumped on the puck and found himself on a wide-open breakaway. He hopped down the ice as fast as he could, cradling the puck on his stick. When he got into the Oak Park slot, he dropped his shoulder to fake a wrist shot, then shifted the puck across his body to his backhand. The Oak Park goalie wasn't fooled. He slid over, staying directly in front of the puck, leaving Jobbi nowhere to shoot. Jobbi did the only thing he could do, flipping the puck high and hoping it would find an opening. It didn't, rebounding instead off the goalie's chest.

Kris Cerps came out of nowhere and grabbed the rebound. The Oak Park goalie dove across the crease and knocked down Kris' shot with the paddle of his stick. It was a miraculous save. An Oak Park defenceman arrived just then and knocked Kris down before he could find the puck and shoot again.

The Oak Park player then pulled the puck in and searched for a place to safely shoot it out of his zone. At that moment, he felt his stick being lifted from behind. Jobbi had circled behind the net and now stole the puck from the defenceman and flipped it into the middle of the Oak Park net before the goalie could regain his feet. A hat trick for Jobbi! Pandemonium followed, both on the ice and in the stands. 3 – 3

Someone threw a warm, fur-lined, winter hat onto the ice. Jobbi recognized it as his uncle's. He picked it up.

A minute later, the buzzer sounded, indicating the end of the third period. Coach Dixon called all the players to the bench. Coach West stood behind him, arms crossed and unhappy. Jobbi checked the giant milk-bottle-shaped clock at the end of the rink. It was seven o'clock.

"All right. Here's how it is, men. Ten minutes of overtime. If no one scores, there'll be a shootout. Don't bother to volunteer. We'll pick the shooters if it gets to that. Starting the OT period will be Jesse's line — then Kris'. Keep the speed up. Let's make the shifts fast and short . . . Anything else Coach West?" The head coach shook his head as though he didn't want to be bothered. "Yes Jobbi. What is it?"

Jobbi's teammates were calling his name and shouting encouragement.

"You're the man, Jobbi."

"Get another one, big guy."

"Keep shooting, Jobbi, keep shooting."

Everyone on the bench was pumped up with excitement — except Coach West, who appeared quite unimpressed.

You've Got To Be Kidding

Stephanie

When it's finally time to set up the ticket table, I feel like I've been working twenty-four hours a day for a week straight. The preparations are going ok — the gym decorations are done and the DJ is almost finished setting up. Most of the teacher and parent supervisors are already here. Ms. Dufault actually volunteered to organize them. Maybe I'm winning her over. Kevin is coming down the hallway, obviously feeling good, singing to himself. Kevin's great. I could really use some of his confidence right now. It's twenty-five after seven.

I was really disappointed when Jobbi told me he was grounded for tonight. I so wanted to cancel the whole thing. But I've been thinking more about Jobbi. He really doesn't have a choice about being here. He got himself into some kind of trouble — something to do with his family. I heard a rumour that his parents might even be in jail in Latvia. Wow. He has to be worried about them. When I think about that, my problems aren't all that huge. I'm the one who was convinced that I could do this, not Jobbi. He thought he was going to help sell tickets at the door, that's all. He has no idea what I was counting on him for.

Once I decided to continue with the dance, my first thought was that without Jobbi I'd have to change everything. Not because I thought I could still make everything work out, but just to try and keep the dance from becoming a total disaster. I thought about maybe making the dance smaller, cancelling the dance contest, ending it at ten-thirty instead of eleven — and maybe worst of all — admitting to Mr. Wickens and Ms. Dufault and my mom that my plans have completely fallen apart, and that — just like they expected — I'd failed. I'm sure if the principal knew what was really going on, he'd want to bring in some security guards.

I should probably be doing all of that, admitting that I've failed . . . but something's been stopping me. It isn't fear of being ridiculed or embarrassed or anything personal like that. The reason I haven't given up like I probably should have is because I don't want to stop believing in Jobbi. That's what's wrong with this whole place. No one believes in anyone else anymore.

My decision doesn't make any sense, I know, and I understand exactly what is at stake for everyone, but I'm the only person in this whole school who knows that there is something special about Jobbi. He definitely is worth the trouble. I've decided that I want to trust in him even if it means me being held responsible for whatever is going to happen tonight. So I haven't changed a thing. It's just the way I've planned it, as though Jobbi is still going to be with me tonight.

Still, now that it's all so close, I'm having a hard time keeping my composure. I feel like I could fall apart any minute. I hope that Kevin remembers to bring his brother's answer ball. Without Jobbi, I still need to come up with some method of using it, since I advertised the oddball dance all over the school.

Kevin plunks the answer ball down in front of me. It isn't black like I thought it would be. It's mauve, and in big cartoon style letters, *Sarcastic Ball* is written across it. I look at Kevin. He shrugs his shoulders and makes a face that says, "Sorry. That's the best I could do." I turn the ball over and check the answer window. Even without me asking a question it reads, "*YOU'VE GOT TO BE KIDDING*."

Just perfect.

Well, at least no one will take the matches seriously. Earlier, Kevin had offered to have his computer club write a matching program that we could use as a back-up plan. I'm really sorry that I didn't take him up on that. Now I'm really nervous. It suddenly hits me that maybe my mother's, my sister's and Ms. Dufault's real concern was that they didn't want to see me end up getting hurt. Why didn't I understand that?

There is already a line-up of maybe fifteen kids waiting to buy tickets. I made a poster for the gym doors, explaining how the oddball dance will work.

"What if we don't want to do that stupid oddball dance?"

It's my on-again-off-again friend, Rena. There is absolutely no way anybody can tell her that she has to do something if she doesn't want to do it.

"You don't have to, Reen. Just tell whoever your partner is that you don't want to dance." I shrug, and try to act like I don't care, but the truth is that the success of this whole dance might come down to what happens at this very moment. Will my idea work or will Rena shoot it down — big time — so that no one else will even give it a try?

Now that I think about it, without Jobbi here, maybe it‘s not such a bad idea to get it over with quickly and ditch the whole plan.

"Who's my partner anyway?"

I take a deep breath. It's all or nothing. I hold the mauve ball up high so everyone in line can see it. "Only the Sarcastic Ball knows." Some kids smile, but not Rena.

"That's stupid."

What Do You Think

Central Middle School

"Hi musz goes now."

"Goes? You mean, leave?" Coach West looked around to the other players with a good effort at a surprised expression on his face. "But we have ten minutes of overtime and then maybe a shootout still to go!"

"Hiam sauhrrry, but mwy frrenzes, hi prromeece tew dem. Hi musz goes."

The players definitely did not want Jobbi to leave.

"Jobbi, you can't go!"

"Overtime, man. O-ver-time!"

"We need another goal! It's our first game!"

"Don't be crazy, dude. You can't leave now."

"Yeah. What could be more important than this game! C'mon!"

It was Jesse, the team captain, who recovered first. "Okay, Guy. Well. Hey — you gotta go, you gotta go. Great game. Good job. You got us this far Jobbi. We'll take it from here . . . No. Leave him alone. Let him go. C'mon, we can do this! Let's go. Let's go. First line. Keep it going, guys!"

The first line hopped over the boards. Jobbi walked off the bench and into the tunnel that led to the dressing rooms. He could feel people watching him. His aunt and uncle, who were in the stands, were concerned that Jobbi had been injured. They made their way to the dressing room to check on him. His aunt stayed outside, but his uncle went in to see if Jobbi was okay. Jobbi was happy to see a friendly face and gave his uncle back his hat. He then asked for a ride to the school. His uncle was relieved to learn that his nephew wasn't injured, and agreed to give him a ride.

"But the game, Jobbi. It is not over yet? No?"

" No, Uncle. But I promised my friends that I'd help them at school."

"Ahh. Ah yes. Friends. Um. Only you can decide that, Jobbi, about your friends. That is how we define the path that we travel in our lives."

Jobbi remembered that his own father had once used those same words. It must be a family saying, he decided.

"That is how your aunt and I came to be in Canada. My friend said that he needed me here. So I came."

Less than twenty-minutes later, Jobbi was at the school. His aunt and uncle watched as he ran in. It was seven-thirty.

Forget About It

Valmiera, Latvia

Christmas was as much fun as Jobbi's Canadian family could make it for him under the circumstances. The trouble was that no one had heard from Jobbi's mother or father or Victor for eight days. Every conversation that started, no matter what it was about, turned into speculation about what was going on with their brother/son/cousin/mother/father/aunt/uncle/sister-in-law/brother-in-law back in Latvia. It wasn't until two days after Christmas that the phone finally rang.

It was Victor.

He was calling to say that Taska and Taylus were on their way to Riga and were hoping, with some help from his parents, to fly from Riga to Canada on the earliest possible flight. Victor's mother dropped the phone and cried out the news so loudly that even those who were still asleep heard her. Everyone in the house rushed to the telephone to listen in. Victor's father didn't have to hear much of the conversation before getting dressed so he could be ready when the travel agency opened.

Victor couldn't explain all of the details on a short telephone call, except to say there had been a complete reversal in Taylus' criminal case, that all the charges had been dropped, that Taylus and Taska were free to go, and that they had decided to join Jobbi in Canada. They had all the papers they would need, thanks to Taska's old uncle, Romerus, who could still pull a few bureaucratic strings.

"And you, Victurus. My son. You will be returning with them?"

" I do not think so, Mom. If you guys have no objection, I think I am going to stay here. I inquired at the University of Riga and I can get into computer engineering with no problem. Plus, they will let me transfer all of my credits from my school. And best of all, it seems like it will be quite a bit less money than it would cost at my old school. Anyway, hey, you guys should think about it and let me know before the fifth of January. That is when I need to register for the new semester. They are willing to let me start before all my transfer papers arrive. And please don't worry about me, Mom. I know what I am doing."

Victor's mother and father barely heard him say goodbye as they embraced one another.

A week before this conversation, Victor had found Aija's bicycle outside the Ceturtais celiens coffee house on Lacple sa St. in Valmiera. It was easy to spot because she had left her silver helmet hanging from the handlebar. She was inside the coffee house talking with two other girls. He went in and sat at another table to watch her, still unsure what he should do. After a little while, the three girls got up to leave and Aija came over to his table. She spoke in Latvian.

"You were looking at me. Staring, actually."

She was smiling. It was a beautiful, generous smile.

"I was? Yes, I was. I'm sorry. I could not help it."

She recognized there was something different about his speech.

"You're not Latvian."

"Yes, I am, or at least I was born here. We moved to Canada when I was five."

"So you are Canadian now. How wonderful. I speak some Canadian, or English I should say. I would love a chance to speak to someone in English. I have to go with my girlfriends right now, but will you be around for long?"

"I could be. I'm not really sure how long."

"I will look for you here. Very soon, I hope. Goodbye . . . Oh, my name is Aija. Yours?"

"I'm Victurus."

She left without him saying anything he wanted to say, and joined her friends outside. He watched them through the door glass. After a brief discussion, she waved goodbye to them and came back into the coffee house.

"Before I sit down, Victurus, you must tell me something truthfully. Do you agree?"

"Yes. I will only tell you the truth."

"Fine. Are you married?"

After hearing that Victor wasn't married, she sat down and explained that she had recently had a very bad experience with a married man who had not told her that he was married. She had decided that she would never, ever have anything to do with a married man again. After that, they spoke only English.

Aija had learned English in her private school and was continuing to learn it at University. The problem for her was that there had been precious little chance to practice it other than by watching American and British films. She thought she might have seen a Canadian film once. Victor found her mesmerizing to listen to. He didn't tell her that he knew all about what she had gone through. She expected him to eventually ask about what her bad experience with a married man had been, so she took the precaution, early on, of telling him that she didn't want to say anything about it until she got to know him better. She then asked Victor to tell her about himself. He told her all about his year-long relationship at school, all the way to its fairly unpleasant conclusion. He used the metaphor of his girlfriend punching him in the stomach to bring the tale to a finish. Aija asked a lot of questions along the way, some very personal things. Victor didn't know if she was actually interested in his story or if she was merely practicing her English. After a couple of hours, they decided to go for a walk past the shops on the street. On their way back to the coffee house, she finally decided to tell Victor about how she had met Boris Michalenkov and the events that followed. When Victor saw how difficult it was for her to speak about it, he stopped her. He admitted that he knew all about it and more.

"You knew. And you didn't say anything? Why? What do you want from me? Never mind. I don't care. Please. Leave me alone."

Before he could tell her about Taylus and about taking his aunt to Aija's home earlier that day, she turned and ran away from him back toward the Ceturtais. She was fast, but Victor was a good runner too. He took off after her. She was surprised to see him running along beside her. He asked her to stop so he could explain something. She pushed him away and ran even faster.

Victor caught up to her once again back at the coffee house where she had parked her bicycle. He kept talking, trying to explain why he was there. Unfortunately he made a real mess of it by trying to speak quickly in Latvian. As it turned out, he had a lot more time than he thought, because Aija was having some trouble opening her bicycle lock. When Victor finally stopped talking to catch his breath, he heard her sniffle. She was crying. That was why she was having trouble with the lock. A key dropped to the pavement. Victor picked it up and opened the lock for her. "I wanted to tell you how much their lives had changed. That is why I wanted to speak with you."

As she walked her bike onto the road, she told him in Latvian that she hadn't understood anything he had said, and that if he did have anything important to say, he should speak slowly in English. Victor felt sure that he would never have another chance to see or talk to her again, so he decided to run beside her on the street, for as long as he could keep up. He started again, in English this time, telling her about Taska and Jobbi going to Canada because they were worried about what might happen to Taska for her part in the affair.

It quickly became difficult to talk and breathe at the same time. Fortunately, the bicycle slowed down. Aija stopped and stood, straddling her bike on the road, hands still on the handlebars and looking straight ahead.

"Taska? What part did Taska have in this affair?"

"She was, I believe, your Matchmaker."

There was a long pause before Aija replied without ever looking at him.

"I had no Matchmaker."

She got up on her peddles and rode off toward her home. Victor no longer tried to follow.

Despite the desperation of his Aunt Taska and Uncle Taylus, Victor couldn't stop thinking about Aija. She obviously didn't know that her meeting with Boris had been arranged. Victor couldn't be sure how this news made her feel, but he suspected it wasn't too good. The last thing he wanted was for her to be hurt again. She had had enough of that already.

Two days after their first meeting, he called her at home. He thought she might hang up or tell him not to call. She didn't. She wanted to talk to him again, face to face. They met at the same coffee house later that day. It turned out that she really had no idea about Taska or Taylus — or even Jobbi — but when she asked, her mother had told her everything.

Aija was horrified that her father had not done anything to help Taylus by now. She promised that she would talk to him as soon as he returned from his trip to Riga. The reason she had wanted to see Victor was to apologize for everything that had happened to his family. She wanted him to tell them so for her. It was clearly important to her that he understood how terribly sorry she was. She also wanted him to know that she had no idea that Taylus had been jailed. Victor believed her. He told her that. When she got up to leave, he impulsively asked her not to go.

"Why?"

He couldn't think of a good reason. He just didn't want her to go yet. She hadn't smiled as she had at their previous meeting.

"Well . . . when you said on the telephone that you would meet me I thought . . . you were asking for another English lesson. So I came here prepared to help you with your English."

"You certainly do not have to do that, Victurus. Not now."

"I know I don't. But . . . but maybe at the same time you can help me with my Latvian?"

"Why do you need to improve your Latvian? You are returning to Canada. No?"

“No. Not necessarily. I was thinking that I might just stay here awhile.” Victor could hardly believe what he was saying.

“But what about your school? Your degree?”

“There is a university here in Latvia somewhere, I believe?”

“Riga has such a school, of course. I attend there.”

“Ah, yes. You did tell me that. Well, what is your opinion? Should I consider changing schools?”

“Why not? The University of Riga is a very good school. Very well respected throughout the world.”

“ Really? Can you tell me about it?”

“ Umm. Perhaps. I have some time.”

Obviously

Kevin

I see Jobbi jogging down the hallway coming toward the gym. He slows down when he hears the clapping from the kids who are excited about finding out who their oddball dance partner will be and waiting to buy a ticket. Stephanie is standing in front of them, showing the Sarcastic Ball I brought from home. I'm not sure if Jobbi realizes how super nervous Stephanie is. And it doesn't help that Rena is in the line glaring at her and threatening to turn everyone against the idea of the oddball dance. Jobbi quietly sits down beside me at the ticket table and looks as happy as I've ever seen him. I pat him on the back.

Stephanie doesn't realize that Jobbi came in behind her. When she turns and sees Jobbi sitting there, she stops in her tracks as though she's seen a ghost, or something even more shocking. She recovers quickly, though, and is obviously trying to stay cool in front of everyone, but she can't hold back this huge happy smile from brightening her whole face. She sits down between us. I think I see her wipe a tear from her cheek with one hand as she passes the Sarcastic Ball to Jobbi with the other. Jobbi must have noticed something too because he tries to peek at her face to make sure that she's okay, but he only ends up making himself woozy and almost falling out of his chair.

Steph is a completely different person now — happy, confident, her nervousness gone, and it's all because Jobbi is here. I'm really glad for him that he still has a chance with her.

I wonder if I'll ever be that important to a girl, if I'll ever get a chance to run into a dance at the last minute and make someone smile the way Stephanie did just now when she saw Jobbi. Maybe Jobbi keeps saying no when I ask him about girls because there isn't anyone who would want to be the girlfriend of a semi-geek like me.

Jobbi tears himself away from Stephanie's face and turns his attention to inspecting the Sarcastic Ball. Stephanie puts her hand over Jobbi's and shows him how to turn it properly and read the answer. Jobbi lets out a yelp of surprise when he sees the words "*WELL, MAYBE*" appear.

"Aakveyaya!"

It doesn't seem to be the words that surprise him. I don't even think he gets sarcasm. I think it's just the novelty of it.

I sell the first ticket to Meghan Campbell, a tall grade-eight girl. Meghan takes her ticket and holds out the back of her left hand for Stephanie to stamp. I hand the Sarcastic Ball to Meghan and tell her how to turn it. She hands it back to me and I pass the answer over to Jobbi to read: "*ASK ME IF I CARE.*" Meghan smiles a little self-consciously. Jobbi frowns at the list of students, then back at the revealed answer. He looks like a bookkeeper double-checking a receipt. He scans the list again — up, down, and even sideways — and makes a note on the corner of the page. He asks me for a ruler, but I don't have one. He points to Stephanie's clipboard, which she passes to him. Jobbi uses the edge of it to draw a line from his note to a column of names. Finally Jobbi's pencil settles on one. He shrugs, indicating that he's done. I look at the name on the list and read it loud enough for everyone in line to hear. "Cory Madari."

Jobbi holds up the Sarcastic Ball to show the message in the window that had created the result. His expression leaves little doubt that he's only following the ball's directions.

Meghan rolls her eyes when she hears her dance partner's name. Cory is short and quite goofy — but she seems to accept the choice — for one dance anyway.

There are more smiles than frowns at the Sarcastic Ball's answers. Jobbi seems to become more impressed by the answer ball each time I hand it to him with a new response. His eyes open wide, as though he can't believe how the Sarcastic Ball can possibly come up with those results. He gets so excited at one point, that he even starts using words I don't recognize, probably stuff from his own language. Once in a while, Jobbi looks at me in total shock, as though he needs someone else to understand how incredible this all is to him. And even though I'm the person who has the most actual experience using that particular answer ball, I have absolutely no idea what is going on between it and Jobbi.

Things sort of calm down when Jobbi and the Sarcastic Ball start working on the same wavelength. Occasionally, he looks over to me and shrugs his shoulders to let me know just how cool he thinks the Sarcastic Ball is.

A few of the kids — well more than a few actually — react like there is no possible way they can dance with the partner the Sarcastic Ball chooses for them. In every case, though, Stephanie suggests they "give it a try — for just one dance." And eventually, because everyone else is going along with it, they do too.

When the players from the hockey team finally show up, Jobbi finds out that the team lost the game in the overtime shootout. None of the players appear to be mad at Jobbi for leaving early. Just the opposite. They're happy that the team played so well and gained their first point of the year for the regulation tie. I guess Jobbi had a lot to do with that. Things are definitely looking up for the team in the future. Jobbi takes less time picking partners for his teammates than for the other kids. I suspect it's because he knows them so well.

After the hockey team goes into the gym, I'm surprised to see Soon Lee suddenly standing right in front of me. Stephanie says, "You came!"

"Yes. My mother asked if my father could use my ticket. He has been working very hard lately and he needs to relax." They smile at one another. Soon Lee is fairly new in the school, but I've noticed her in my life skills class. She seems shy, but I don't think she really is. Like me. I look around to see who she came with and I can't see anyone. She must have come alone. Not many kids would do that. She turns the answer ball and hands it back to me. Jobbi looks quickly at the answer, "*OBVIOUSLY,*" but instead of showing me the name on the list so I can say it, he reads the name out loud himself: "Kaveen Vundarrroaf."

Soon Lee smiles. I can't believe it. And she smiles right at me, just like she's totally happy that I'm her partner. I thought she'd be disappointed or roll her eyes, but she didn't. Things kinda get blurry, so I wipe my face with my sleeve and push the cash box over to Stephanie. Soon Lee gives me her hand and we walk into the gym together.

Not A Chance

Stephanie

When I turn around and see Jobbi sitting at the ticket table, I can't believe that he's real at first. I mean, even though I had prepared as though he was going be there, I never really expected him to actually show up. When I pass him the Sarcastic Ball and touch his hand. I'm so relieved that I almost start bawling. I know that everything is totally going to be good.

Jobbi is great with the Sarcastic Ball — so good that no one even asks how he does it, how he uses an answer from the Sarcastic Ball to find a dance partner.

Once most of the kids have arrived and the music has started, I count the money in the cash box and take it to the office to be put into the safe. Vice-Principal Wickens is there. He asks me how the dance is going. I have to tell him that I actually don't know because I've been way too busy to go into the gym. Mr. Wickens is really edgy. He probably has visions of kids fighting or maybe even rioting. I know he's trying his best to trust the volunteer supervisors, but it's not their jobs on the line if something goes wrong.

I trust Jobbi, but I still can't help being a little worried about trouble. I so want to go straight into the gym and check things out, but decide that I'd better go back to the table and finish things up there first.

When I get to the far end of the hall, I see Jobbi talking with Paula. She's the girl the Dixie Road gang were planning to mess up. Even from this far away, I can tell by the way she's dressed that guys will have to check her out, whether they're interested in her or not. I can't help feeling a little jealous. I have an idea what she and Jobbi are talking about.

Only half the kids actually get a chance to have Jobbi, or the Sarcastic Ball — or both together — pick a dance partner for them. That's because the other half of the kids are already chosen as partners. It's kind of spooky when someone who's already been chosen as a dance partner, shows up at the ticket table. Jobbi just sits there in this little frozen trance, like one of those mechanical fortune tellers you see on the midway at the exhibition — before you put the money in, that is. It's because he already knows that he isn't needed. He also knows that me and Kevin can easily look up the person's name on the list and see who's written down beside it. I don't mind, because I realize it helps Jobbi to concentrate.

Paula is on her way into the gym when she suddenly turns around. She looks upset and stomps back to the ticket table — and Jobbi.

I start to run.

Get A Clue

Paula

I wasn't intending to go to the dance at first. It seemed too dangerous for me. Everyone who wanted to get me would definitely be there. Then I found out that my mother and stepdad were going to his company Christmas party that same night. That would leave me home alone with Dylan. I didn't want that either. I decided to take my chances with the dangers at school. Hopefully, there'd be someone there to break things up if I got jumped. And if there wasn't, then I'd have the Vikov.

I knew all the girls were planning to wear dresses. If everybody was going to talk about me anyway, I decided that I might as well give them something to talk about. I borrowed the shortest, most revealing, black cocktail dress my mother had in her closet. It only took a few pins to make it fit the way I wanted it to. I also borrowed a pair of her patent-leather heels.

I went alone, because no one would want to go with me anyway. It was a very cold, dark night. I was beginning to think that I saw things in the shadows along the way. I put the heels on when I got to school and threw my walking shoes in my locker. The dance had already started by the time I arrived.

The other hallways were completely deserted and only every third light was on along the way. I knew that if I got jumped here, I'd be completely on my own. I held my bag in my right hand and kept my left hand inside on the Vikov's handle.

I was almost at the gym before I heard any music. It didn't seem very loud for some reason. There was only one person at the ticket table, that crazy Russian guy, Jobbi. He was in a couple of my classes, but I'd never talked to him before. He was definitely one of the few guys who didn't show any interest in what I wore to school every day. He took my ticket without saying anything, then put a stamp on my hand and pointed toward the gym door. Something about the whole night so far seemed wrong to me. What if there really was no dance? What if this was a setup with the Dixie Road girls waiting for me inside the gym? When I started to think about it, it didn't sound so crazy. Even this Jobbi guy could be in on it for all I knew. I started to panic. I decided that I wasn't going anywhere until I was sure it was safe.

"Hey, what about that sign on the door? Like, *who* do I dance with?"

Again, he didn't say anything to me, and again, he pointed at the gym doors. That made me angry. I'd had it with people pushing me around, setting me up. Then out of nowhere, that freaked-out Stephanie chick rushes up behind me. So, that was it! It was her and the Dixie Roaders who'd planned all of this. Their big chance to get me. There was no way I was going down without a fight. I found the Vikov in my bag and pushed the trigger, but I was nervous and not holding the handle properly. The blade sliced the pad of my thumb as it sprang out. I heard the gym doors open. That would be the gang coming to get in on the action. I was determined to get as many of them as I could before they got me — starting with Miss Stephanie Stresscase.

"Hey, there she is! My partner. I was starting to think you weren't comin'. Wow! You look great, Paula. Are you ready for some dancing?"

"Huh? What . . . ?" I recognized the voice right away. I let go of the knife and turned around. Jesse Twerndon was here. I felt dizzy. Like when I forget to eat for a couple of days.

"Hey, Paula. Are you ok? Oh, wow. Your hand. There's blood on it. Let me see that. Anyone got a hanky or something?"

"Don't worry about it, Jesse. I'm ok. It's only my thumb. Ugh, I might have some tissue in my bag?" With the blood and all, I forgot for that one second about the knife that was still in there. Before I could stop him Jesse reached inside my bag and I saw the expression on his face change. He hesitated for a couple of seconds. There was a tiny click that no one else except me would have recognized, the knife's blade being retracted. He found some tissue, closed my bag and looked into my face. Tears came to my eyes. I tried to stop them. He gave me the tissue to hold against the cut. We continued to look at each other for what seemed like minutes, but was probably only a few seconds. Then he reached up with another tissue and caught a tear that had trickled down onto my chin.

I kept the pressure on my sliced thumb while Jesse scooped my bag under one of his arms and put his other arm around my shoulders. He led me through the gym doors and into the dance. My head was light and I felt a bit disoriented, as though I was in some kind of dream, or maybe, just waking up from one.

In Your Dreams

Stephanie

Just as I get to the table, Jesse, Paula's oddball dance partner, comes out of the gym. I don't know what's happening now, but it looks like Paula almost fainted. Earlier, when Jobbi had told Jesse that Paula was his dance partner, Jesse hadn't even seemed surprised. He just shrugged. He'd come out of the gym a few times since then, looking for her. I think he was worried that she might not show up. I wonder how Paula dancing with Jesse would go over with the Dixie Roaders. Whatever. Jesse can handle it. Besides, The Dixie Roaders have their own dance partners.

Jobbi tells me about Paula cutting her hand. He wipes up a bit of blood from the table. I see a few drops on the floor too. I can't look at it because it makes me feel sick, but to Jobbi, it's no big deal. When he finishes that, he starts working with the Sarcastic Ball again and making some calculations on the student list. I have no idea what he's working so hard at. Finally he finds what he's looking for and becomes quite excited.

"Stayfoonie. Loouk!"

He holds up the Sarcastic Ball so I can see. It reads, "*IN YOUR DREAMS*."

"Chyou sees?"

He wants me to understand something. I only nod, 'cause I'm not sure what it is that he is showing me. He points at his chest, then to the list of student names. There are only a few that aren't marked as having a partner for the oddball dance. I lean over the list to read the name he's found . . . Stephanie T. Horner.

I throw my arms around his neck and hug him. Hard. I can't help it.

"Aakveyaya!"

He hugs me back.

ARTHUR JACK STEWART lives in Victoria, British Columbia. His writing has appeared in journals and magazines such as *Island Writer Magazine* and the *Winnipeg Sun*. His play *Bad Rabbit Winter* came second in the 1991 CBC Playwriting Competition. This is his first book.